'We... ...d.
'It's so good to see you again.'

—

He ...
sou...
How could she have forgotten this?

Just for a second she wondered what things might have been like if she and Ben had carried on with their plans and… This was madness!

This was no good; she had to get a grip on herself! She was a nurse, a professional, not easily swayed by emotion. Not now, anyway. Not after the past few weeks. Whatever life threw at her—she could cope!

Both were silent a moment, staring at each other. And slowly, silently, she slid back into today, into the real world. But she couldn't help wondering what he had felt. For a moment she had thought she could see in his eyes something of her own feelings. But that was then and this was now. She looked at him and marvelled ... ...ed. Had she too cha...

Gill Sanderson, aka Roger Sanderson, started writing as a husband-and-wife team. At first Gill created the storyline, characters and background, asking Roger to help with the actual writing. But her job became more and more time-consuming, and he took over all of the work. He loves it!

Roger has written many Medical™ Romance books for Harlequin Mills & Boon. Ideas come from three of his children—Helen is a midwife, Adam a health visitor, Mark a consultant oncologist. Weekdays are for work; weekends find Roger walking in the Lake District or Wales.

Recent titles by the same author:

THE MIDWIFE AND THE SINGLE DAD

BY
GILL SANDERSON

MILLS & BOON®
Pure reading pleasure™

First published in Great Britain 2009
Harlequin Mills & Boon Limited,
Eton House, 18-24 Paradise Road, Richmond, Surrey TW9 1SR

ISBN: 978 0 263 86839 5

Set in Times Roman 10½ on 12¼ pt
03-0409-49195

Printed and bound in Spain
by Litografia Rosés, S.A., Barcelona

THE MIDWIFE
AND THE
SINGLE DAD

For Steven James, a real alpha male

CHAPTER ONE

ALICE MUIR could have done without this.

'Excuse me, but is there a doctor on the plane?'

Alice looked quickly around the cabin. There were a number of concerned faces but no hands were raised. She could feel the embarrassment of the other passengers, many of them staring downwards to avoid the hostess's eyes. Alice wanted to do the same.

The hostess was young. Trying, as trained, to keep her voice calm but not succeeding. After a moment she spoke again. 'Well, is there anyone with any kind of medical knowledge?'

It was only a small passenger plane, flying short routes across Scotland, there weren't many passengers. They would be lucky if one was a doctor. Around her she could feel people stirring uneasily, looking as if to accuse their fellows of being doctors and not owning up to the fact.

Alice didn't need this. Being ready to help had resulted in her… She was a midwife and a registered children's nurse, she was not a doctor. Certainly she had some medical skills. But not being insured and trying to help outside the strict limits of her professional role had caused her to be in this mess. Could she trust the people she was being asked to deal with? Being helpful, relying on trust had just caused her to lose her job. Had also caused her to become disengaged—though that was probably a good thing. In fact, relying on trust was the cause of her coming back to Soalay—the island of her birth. Alice felt she could trust no one.

The silence lengthened and Alice sighed. She just couldn't sit here if there was someone she might be able to help. Reluctantly, she raised her hand then stood and walked towards the front of the cabin. She saw the hostess's face light up with hope.

Speaking as quietly as she could, she said, 'My name's Alice Muir, I'm not a doctor or a nurse I'm a midwife and a qualified children's nurse. I've got some nursing knowledge but it's nearly all to do with children.'

In fact, she knew that her general nursing knowledge was quite extensive. But it was as well to explain things clearly from the beginning. 'What's the problem?'

The hostess looked at her happily. 'I'm Angela. I've been on a first-aid course but I've never had to do anything. I just don't know. I'm sure you'll be able to help.'

'Well, let's see.' Alice could feel the curious eyes of the passengers on her, wondering who she was, what she was able to do. She didn't like it. Too many people had been studying her recently, hoping to see her reactions. Still, she had volunteered. She had to do what she could.

Angela led her to a seat at the front of the cabin.

There was a woman slumped against the tiny window. She was perhaps in her sixties, a thin woman with a lined, pale face, dressed in an odd-looking long black coat. No one was sitting next to her.

Angela whispered, 'She seemed very nervous when she got on so I put her in a seat on her own. She doesn't speak much English—I think she's Polish or something East European like that. I think this is her first flight ever. She was frightened. I kept an eye on her, but she refused to have a drink or anything, just shook her head. Then I saw that she was unconscious. She is unconscious, isn't she? Not just asleep?'

'Sort of half and half,' Alice said. She put her head close to the woman's, said in her kindest voice, 'Hi, there, are you all right? Is there anything I can get you? I'm a nurse.'

There was a reaction of some sort. The woman didn't open her eyes but mumbled something in a language that certainly wasn't English. And then her voice just trailed away.

Alice sighed. There wasn't much to go on. She checked the woman's wrists to see if there was any kind of bracelet with medical details on it. No. She opened the neck of the black coat to see if there was a locket there with the same information. No again. Alice sighed again.

The next step was to open the woman's handbag. There were pills there in a little plastic container—but unfortunately the prescription was in Polish. Alice sighed. No simple answer here.

The usual vital ABC check—airways, breathing, circulation. All seemed more or less in order. But the breathing was shallow, the pulse light, the skin cold and clammy. Alice looked at the woman, shook her head in dismay. She didn't have the usual array of diagnostic tools and she wasn't a… Then something struck her. 'You say she refused a drink?' she asked Angela.

'Yes. And we're supposed to encourage passengers to drink—not alcohol, that is…'cos…'

''Cos of dehydration. I don't suppose you know if she had a drink while she was waiting to catch the plane?'

'Well, I did see her before she boarded and there was no drink in her hand. She was just sitting in a corner by herself. She looked ill then.'

'Go and get me the most sugar-laden soft drink you can find.'

Now, there was something that Angela could recognise. 'Sugar! You think she's—'

'The drink, Angela!'

Angela fetched it. Alice checked the sugar content on the tin and winced. This stuff would rot children's teeth faster than acid. But for the moment it could be what was wanted. She took the woman's head in her arm, leaned it back and then dribbled the sweet fruit drink between the half-open lips. Reflexively, the woman choked, and then had to swallow. Alice poured more of the drink into the now open mouth—and the woman moved. Her eyes flashed open.

Alice had heard of this but had never actually seen it. The woman was a diabetic and, presumably because of worry, had not controlled her sugar intake. But the speed at which a diabetic suffering from hypoglycaemia, low blood sugar, could recover was amazing. Two minutes later the woman was sitting upright, clutching the can of drink in her own hands. She smiled and said something to Alice and Angela.

'I think we're being thanked,' said Alice.

'I'm glad we didn't have to make an emergency landing,' said Angela. 'There's only mountains below.'

The immediate emergency was over, there was now time to think. Alice said, 'This woman isn't making this trip on her own. There must be someone waiting for her. Can the pilot radio ahead and check at the airport? Broadcast on the PA system. Is there anyone waiting for their grandmother—possibly Polish?'

Angela looked at Alice, open-eyed. 'I should have thought of that,' she said. 'But I'll see to it at once.'

She came back ten minutes later. 'Yes, there is a Polish family waiting for a relation and, yes, she is diabetic and they're worried and they want to know if the plane can fly any faster. But the pilot says it can't.'

'It's an exciting life, being an air hostess,' said Alice. 'You carry on with your work and I'll sit with her.'

It was straightforward after that. The woman held Alice's hand with a grip like a vice as they landed, her eyes were screwed shut, and she muttered a set of what Alice guessed were prayers. Then Angela asked all the passengers to keep their seats while paramedics came on board and escorted the ill lady off the plane. On a stretcher. Alice was thanked by the plane's captain and asked if she'd like to be thanked by the Polish family. She said, no, she didn't want any fuss. Then she saw that both the captain and Angela were a bit disappointed. She had to remember, this was island

Scotland, not London. People held together more. This was a community.

She only had one wheelie bag with her, the rest of her belongings would be coming later. She took a taxi down through the small town to the harbour, calculating that it would be only an hour before the ferry left, she'd be able to get on board.

She stared out of the taxi window, looking at the changes that had been made. She hadn't been here for fifteen years, there had been progress. For a start, the plane service was new. In the past she had travelled by ferry and then train. And the place looked…brighter.

The taxi was able to drive right onto the quay, and then the driver insisted on carrying her bag onto the ferry. Not the kind of service she'd expect in London. She found herself a seat near the bows, fetched herself a mug of coffee and then sat and relaxed. Or tried to. She had to admit she felt a little better already. And the incident of the plane had, for a while, taken her mind off her own problems.

The last few days—the last few weeks—had been full of stress. But now things should be different. She sat there, happy in the slight breeze of sea air. It smelled good, so different from the fumes of London. She heard the screaming of the gulls, the soft, Western Isles accent. Again, different from polyglot London. And last of all there was the view. For once the sea was blue. The mountains behind the town were green-grey and they were beautiful.

She turned her head and looked out to sea. In the

distance she could see the smudge of land that was Soalay. She was returning to the island of her birth, seeking refuge for her battered life. She hadn't been back for fifteen years and now she wondered why not.

She had been happy there—but like all young people had felt the need to move on, to see what the big exciting world had to offer her. Well, she had certainly found that out. But why never back to Soalay? She couldn't visit her parents. Shortly after she had left they had emigrated to New Zealand, to live with her older brother. And somehow there had never seemed to be time to return.

But she was back now. She had been happy here, perhaps she would be happy again. Perhaps the island would calm her, wake her from what had been the living nightmare of the past few weeks. She hoped so.

She felt the rumble and vibration of engines, heard the shouts of men on the quayside, the splash of ropes dropping into the water. The ferry eased away from the quayside, threaded its slow way through the moored fishing boats. They cleared the harbour mouth, she felt the gentle rise and fall of the ship as they headed out to sea.

The excitement of the start of a new journey. She was going home—but only for a year. She knew she could not run from memories for ever.

Just what had she let herself in for?

The journey was over all too quickly. Now the other travellers on the ferry were getting ready to disembark, gathering their shopping bags together, calling for their children. Alice didn't feel like moving. She had been calm on the ferry, but now she was wondering what she had done. Was she happy or sad? Was this a courageous career move or was it a mad dash back to a refuge because she hadn't made a success of life in London? She wasn't sure. Which seemed to be her constant attitude of mind.

The ferry slowed, cautiously made its way into the tiny harbour. People were waiting on the jetty, ready to meet friends and relations. Alice looked at them carefully, there were one or two that she thought she recognised. A boy who'd been in her year at school. And a girl who had been three or four classes behind Alice, so she was three or four years younger. Now she clutched the hand of a little boy and was pushing a pram. Two children? Well, it was possible.

How many people would remember her?

Then a sudden shock, far greater than she had ever anticipated. There was…there was Ben. Ben Cavendish. Broad and tall and now so close. He saw her just as she saw him—he smiled and waved at her. Ben was the GP she would be working for—no, working with. She was a professional in her own right.

Fifteen years ago they had been teenage sweethearts. In love in that breathless way that only teenagers could experience and sure that their love would last. And they had made plans—which had come to nothing.

How their lives had changed in fifteen years! Alice waved back. But somehow she couldn't manage a smile.

There was the usual bustle of coming alongside, ropes were thrown, the companionways slid over the side, the little ship was made fast to the jetty. People moved to get ashore quickly and for a while she lost sight of him in the crowds.

She didn't want to rush ashore herself. Emotions, feelings she couldn't identify, suddenly confused her. She hadn't expected to feel like this. Memories of fifteen years ago suddenly seemed like yesterday, she was hurting now as she had hurt then.

There was the coastguard's hut they had hidden behind! Exactly the same. For a moment she remembered the heat of his body as he'd held her, remembered the touch of his lips on hers. She was on the very same ferry that had carried her away from him.

Life had been simpler then. She could see it might get difficult now. How would she get on with Ben? She had just seen him smile at her but that didn't mean that he was really pleased to see her. There could be problems. For a moment she wondered about staying on the ferry, going back to the mainland. Coming here had been a lunatic idea and she ought to change her mind before things got worse. Perhaps she could go and book a ticket at once.

Then she decided that this was just the result of fatigue. The past few days, weeks had been a rollercoaster of problems, the effects were catching up on her. And this was only a new job!

The crowds had lessened now, she turned to pick up her bag. And behind her a voice said, 'Hi, Alice. I'll take that.'

She turned, speechless. She knew her mouth had dropped open, she couldn't close it. Ben! He must have come up a companionway to greet her. Here he was in front of her and fifteen years fell away and she was a hapless eighteen-year-old girl again, saying goodbye to her boyfriend. She'd loved him so much!

Both were silent a moment, staring at each other. And slowly, silently she slid back into today, into the real world. But she couldn't help wondering what he had felt. For a moment she had thought she could see in his eyes something of her own feelings. But that had been then and this was now. She looked at him and marvelled at how little he had changed. Had she too changed so little?

His body was heavier, muscle had replaced the slimness of youth. By contrast, his face was thinner. He had lost his adolescent cheeks, he was now a man. There were lines by his eyes and to the side of his mouth, it was the face of a man who had seen something of life. It wasn't entirely a happy face.

But his eyes were the same and what eyes they were! They changed what had been a normal pleasant face into something memorable. They were large, grey, sometimes they seemed to have a tint of the sea's green in them. To Alice, it had always been possible to know what he was thinking, just by looking into his eyes. She remembered the saying—the eyes were the windows of the soul. That was so right.

But now his eyes had changed. If they were windows then they were shuttered, she couldn't tell his thoughts. There was something hidden there, something wary. She wondered what.

'Welcome home, Alice,' Ben said. 'It's good to see you again.'

He had always had a soft voice. And now the sound

of it nearly brought her to tears again. How could she had forgotten this?

Just for a second she wondered what things might have been like if she and Ben had carried on with their plans and… This was madness! She had been told some time ago that Ben was a married man! So Alice had to content herself with the thought that Ben's wife was a very lucky woman. Alice envied her.

This was no good, she had to get a grip on herself! She was a nurse, a professional, not easily swayed by emotion. Not now, anyway. Not after the past few weeks. Whatever life threw at her—she could cope!

He had greeted her when she had been half turned way. But now she had straightened and they were looking at each other face to face. And it seemed that he too was struck silent. But Alice struggled a moment and managed a reply. 'It's good to see you too, Ben.'

Awkwardly she held out her hand. Wasn't this how colleagues greeted each other? He took her hand in both of his, and to her surprise pulled her towards him, kissed her on the cheek. She felt the slight roughness of his skin. She remembered that too and a dart of recognition pierced her. Even as a seventeen-year-old he had had to shave every day.

Perhaps he noticed her surprise. 'We are to be colleagues and we've got to work together,' he said gently. 'But we're also old friends and so we're entitled to kiss each other when we meet.'

'Old friends,' she agreed. 'And it's good to be back, Ben.' She knew her voice was hoarse but there was nothing she could do about it. And, in an action that surprised her as much as him, she leaned forward and kissed him in turn. Quickly, of course. But on the lips. And the two of them looked at each other in surprise again.

Alice tried not to show it but felt a definite sense of relief. She and Ben were going to get on. She had wondered how she would cope if for some reason Ben blamed her for them having to part all those years ago. But it hadn't been her fault, not really. Or had it? She just didn't know.

Time to move. He grabbed her bag, lifted it easily. Ben Cavendish was not a man to trundle a wheelie bag. 'You're a few days early,' he told her. 'The trust told me that you were coming to settle in before starting work but I'm afraid we're not quite ready for you yet. Your clinic is more or less done and most of the supplies have been shipped in. But the builders have to put the finishing touches to your flat. There's some decorating to do and, more to the point, some plumbing to fix.'

He was leading her down the companionway, swinging her case as if it were a toy. 'Now, that's my vehicle.' He pointed to a decidedly battered-looking Land Rover. He led her to it, then stopped and looked cautiously at her.

'So there'll be nowhere for you to sleep for a while. We could find a bed-and-breakfast place for you or a room in a hotel, but I wondered...' He hesitated then quickly said, 'I wondered if you'd like to stay with me, just for a few days until the work is finished.'

The idea shocked her, she felt her heart begin to beat faster. Stay with Ben? She had not expected this. It would be...

Her doubts must have shown on her face, because he rushed on, 'Sorry, it's a silly idea, there'll be no difficulty in finding you a place and—'

'Wouldn't your wife mind me staying?' Alice had to ask.

His reply was clipped, remote. 'I have no wife. I'm afraid we've parted. She's been gone for quite a while and the divorce is now through.'

It took Alice a moment to get over the shock. Then she gazed at Ben's face but she couldn't read him any more, his face seemed expressionless. Was there sadness when he talked about his long-gone wife? Did he miss her, still love her? Alice just could not tell. So she contented herself by asking, 'So you live as a bachelor?'

A more cheerful reply. 'No. I have a housekeeper, Mrs McCann. She lives in and she's marvellous.'

Ben, divorced? It was all too much for Alice to take in. She knew she had to be careful here but she did so want to know more. 'It must be hard, getting divorced,' she ventured. 'Pretty painful.'

His reply was curt. Obviously he didn't want to talk about it. 'It was painful. And ultimately unnecessary. Perhaps if things had been different, if I'd have been a different kind of man…'

Unnecessary? Did that mean that he still had feelings for his ex-wife? And why should he want to be a different kind of man? But by the bleak look in Ben's eyes Alice guessed that further questions would be resented. In time she was determined to know more, but for the moment something more pleasant. She thought she had recognised the name of the housekeeper. 'Mrs McCann?

Mother of Elsie McCann who we were at school with? She used to run the post office?'

'That's the one. Being my housekeeper is only a temporary thing, she's got bad arthritis and she'll move in with her daughter in a few months. I'll have to find someone else then. She'll be hard to replace but people will rally round.'

Alice remembered this. On the island people did rally round. This was not like the isolation of London.

She realised she had not answered his question. Well, she hadn't been expecting it. It was all a bit bewildering, perhaps she ought to think about it first. Was it really a good idea and what if…? But even as she wondered she found herself saying, 'If you're sure I'll be no bother, then I'd really like to stay with you. But only for a while. I don't want to be any trouble.'

Then she felt a slight sense of shock. She hadn't intended to agree so quickly, she had intended to consider the idea first. But the words had just seemed to come out of their own accord. She felt apprehensive—but apprehensive about what? Perhaps she was still a bit tired.

'So it's settled, then,' he said cheerfully. 'Good. Climb in.'

He threw her bag into the back seat and she found herself next to him as they drove off. She liked sitting high above the other vehicles.

She just had to say it. 'This is a bit different from the bicycles we used to ride together.'

'Very different. But the Land Rover is very efficient.'

She got the impression that for the moment he didn't

want to remember their youth together and he was silent as they negotiated the busy streets around the harbour. So she looked round. Changes in the past fifteen years? There had been quite a few. The shops seemed busier, there was now a supermarket. Some of the older, almost derelict buildings had been renovated. And there were more people on the streets.

'Things have changed,' she said to him. 'And there seem to be more younger people around.'

He nodded. 'The economy is taking off. Partly European money. The place is coming to life again, more babies are being born here and more young people are staying. Which is why we need this new clinic you're going to set up. We hope not to have to send for the helicopter so often, we want to be able to deal with our own medical emergencies.'

'Right. Sounds good.' Then she was silent again and soon they were out of town. The place had grown—but not too much. It was still only a small town. Memories came crowding back, she realised how much she had missed being here.

'So you have Mrs McCann as a housekeeper? Do you really need someone to look after you? I would have thought you quite capable of looking after yourself.' Alice had thought about this, felt herself quite surprised.

His answer was grim. 'I could lead the bachelor life. In some ways I would much prefer it. But I need someone to look after Fiona in the days and at nights when I'm called out.'

'Fiona?'

'Fiona, my daughter. She's nearly five.'

'You have a daughter?'

'I do, and she's the centre of my life. I love her.'

Alice had never expected this, this was the greatest shock so far. She had coped—or had expected to cope—with Ben having a wife. Though there had been a slight feeling of disappointment. But a daughter? Well, if a wife, why not a daughter? It seemed eminently under-standable. But Alice just hadn't thought about it.

Ben had a child. She did not, though once she had expected one. The thought hurt.

CHAPTER TWO

SHE had noticed the alteration in his voice when he'd spoken of Fiona. There was tenderness, obvious love. He had never spoken to her like that, even when they had been close as teenagers. But Alice grudgingly had to admit that they had been much younger then. Their capacity for emotions might not have been limited but their ability to express them certainly had been.

'It'll be nice to meet your daughter,' she said, hoping that her voice didn't betray exactly what she was feeling. Not that she was quite sure herself what she felt. Surely not jealousy? She decided to change the subject. 'Where are we going? You don't live in your parents' old house, do you?'

He shook his head. 'I wanted to get a bit out of town but be handy. So I bought a place and spent far too much money on having it renovated. But now I love it. Wait and see, I think you'll love it too.'

As he spoke they turned off the main road—not that it was a main road by London standards—and onto something much more narrow. There was only space for one vehicle, with the occasional passing place. She remembered the road—and then she guessed where they were going. 'Ben! We're going to Taighean dhe Gaoithe!'

'We are. It's my home now.'

Taighean dhe Gaoithe was Gaelic for Face of the Storm. It was an apt name. Two minutes later she saw it. There was a dip in the cliffs and there, facing the beach, was the house. She knew that it had been built in Victorian times as a hunting lodge. It was in weathered grey stone, it looked tough but beautiful. She realised what a wonderful position it was in—it was private but only twenty minutes' drive from town. And the view!

'We used to come here when no one was in and wonder what it was like inside.'

His reply was curt again. 'We did. I remember well.'

He didn't seem very keen to remember their old times together. But for the moment Alice didn't care. 'It seems odd, driving along here with you,' she said. 'It's odd because it seems so familiar. As if the past fifteen years had just slipped away. When we parted we thought that it would only be a matter of weeks before we met again. And yet… I'm sorry we lost touch, Ben. And we had such plans. It was my fault.'

He shrugged. 'Fault doesn't come into it. We were young, we didn't know what we wanted, didn't know what life was like. Then we learned.'

'We certainly did.' It sounded as if Ben had had as hard a time as she had. Such a pity! She decided to remain silent for a while, take in the view.

Eventually the car pulled up at the front of the house. The great oak front door opened and a little girl ran out.

'Daddy, Daddy, Daddy!' Ben jumped out of the Land Rover, ran to meet his daughter. He picked her up, swung her round until she laughed with joy. She was dressed in red shorts and a T-shirt with a giraffe pictured on it. She had the same thick dark hair as her father and, best of all, she had her father's grey eyes. Too early to tell—she still had the chubbiness of childhood—but Alice thought she was going to be a beauty. A beauty like her mother? Alice thought, and was surprised at the irritation this idea caused her.

Now Ben put his daughter down, held her hand and led her towards the vehicle. Feeling unsure, Alice stepped out of the car and waited. Why was she nervous about meeting a child? She had met many after all. When the two got closer she bent down and smiled.

'Fiona, this is an old friend of mine,' Ben said. 'I'd like you to call her Auntie Alice.'

'Hello, Auntie Alice,' Fiona said doubtfully, after a pause.

'Hello, Fiona. Aren't you a lovely little girl.' On impulse Alice leaned forward and kissed Fiona on the cheek. Then she frowned. Even in this summer weather, the cheek felt warm. Too warm? But, then, Fiona had obviously been running about.

'And this is Mrs McCann,' Ben went on. 'I'm sure you remember her.'

Alice stood, took the older woman's outstretched hand. 'I do indeed. Mrs McCann, it's Alice Muir. I'm sure you remember all those heavy medical books you used to get for me from the mainland.'

'Yes, I remember them. And I'm pleased to see

you've made good use of them. Alice, it's good to see you back home after all these years.'

'How's Fiona been all day, Mrs McCann?' Ben asked.

Mrs McCann frowned. 'The better for seeing you. But she's been a bit out of sorts. And it's got worse as the day's gone on. Quiet, you know. And she's not eaten much at all. Not like her.'

Ben picked up his daughter and she nuzzled into his neck. Alice leaned forward, put her hand on her forehead. She looked at Ben, raised her eyebrows. 'A bit feverish?' she asked. 'Is there anything going round?'

Ben shrugged. 'It's summertime. There's lots of visitors, trippers, they bring business to the island but they also bring their germs with them. We often have an increase in minor illnesses among the locals. You're a children's nurse, what do you think I should do?'

She was pleased he had asked her opinion. 'Get her to take things easy, no excitement or undue running about. Plenty of fluids, plenty of rest, don't worry too much if her appetite goes. At night, perhaps children's paracetamol to calm her fever. If it only started this morning, don't be surprised if things get a bit worse.'

'Just what I would have said.' Ben grinned. 'Come on, let's go inside. I'll get your case.'

'You carry Fiona and I'll get the case. She doesn't want you to put her down.'

Fiona obviously agreed. 'Want to be carried,' she said, wrapping her arms firmly round her father's neck. Their love for each other was so obvious that Alice felt a slight touch of envy. Nobody loved her like that.

* * *

Alice loved the inside of the house. Years before, when they had been certain the house had been uninhabited, she and Ben had crept up to the windows, tried to peer through the gaps in the drawn curtains. All they had been able to manage had been glimpses of ornate woodwork, fancy plastered ceilings. Now she could see it in all its splendour. The woodwork, the plasterwork were still there. But the rest of the décor was in light pastel shades and the furniture was modern. It made a wonderful contrast.

Alice had obviously been expected as there was a bedroom with its own en suite waiting for her. 'I gather that you've been travelling more than a bit today,' Mrs McCann said. 'If you'd like to freshen up there's towels there ready. If you want to come downstairs in half an hour or so, we can all have a cup of tea with Fiona before Dr Cavendish puts her to bed.'

'I'd like that,' Alice said. 'And, yes, I am feeling a bit travel worn.'

She had a quick shower and noted approvingly that the Victorian plumbing had been replaced by something modern. There was even a hairdryer—now, that was thoughtful. Though she had packed one of her own. Now, what to wear? She had travelled in jeans and a light jacket, trainers on her feet, an outfit more practical than elegant. Perhaps it was time for a change. She found a pretty floral summer dress, treated herself to a touch of make-up. She wasn't really sure why. She just felt like being…not attractive but smart.

The four of them sat round a large table in the kitchen. There was tea and buttered scones for the three adults, a small meal for Fiona. And Fiona had got worse in the past half-hour. She would hardly eat, she was argumentative, tearful. She didn't know whether she wanted to sit on her father's lap or in her chair. She had to be moved from one to the other.

'She's not usually like this,' Ben whispered. 'She can be a sweet child.'

Alice smiled. 'I'm a children's nurse. I know what to expect. May I hold her for a while?'

So Fiona was transferred to Alice's lap and was promptly sick all over Alice's new dress.

Ben and Mrs McCann looked on in horror. 'Fiona, are you all right?' Ben asked anxiously, and held out his arms for his child.

Alice shook her head warningly. 'Leave her with me,' she said. 'There's nothing serious about this. I should have known better, should have expected this. Now, if there's an apron I can borrow, I'll take her to the bathroom.'

The phone rang in the hall. 'It's Wednesday evening,' Ben said gloomily. 'It's supposed to be my evening off.' He went to answer it.

Mrs McCann was sponging down Alice's dress. 'If you're all right holding her for a while, I'll go and fetch the wee one's pyjamas,' she said. 'Then we'll see to that dress.'

'Let me take her to the bathroom and undress her,' Alice said. 'Where is it?'

Mrs McCann led her down the corridor.

Being sick had quietened Fiona. She slumped peacefully on Alice's shoulder and Alice overheard Ben's conversation. 'Another fit, you say? Fell and cut his head…? Stopped the bleeding? Yes, I'll come out and have a look. But don't worry too much, Mrs Melling. I'm sure things will be fine…'

A moment later he came into the bathroom, just as Alice turned on the taps. 'Alice, how do you think Fiona is?' he whispered.

Alice poured water over the little girl's head. 'I suspect it's just a minor upset. It'll be over very quickly. You're a doctor, you should know that.'

'I do know it. But if you had a child of your own, you'd know how hard it is to be the detached medical observer.'

'I guess so,' she said. She didn't have a child of her own. He wasn't to know just how much this remark hurt her.

'This is not the way I wanted to greet you,' he went on, 'but I have to go. One of my patients is an epileptic—he's hurt his head and his mother worries overmuch. I'll have to go and see. It's a pity really. I'll have to ask Mrs McCann to babysit. Usually on Wednesday she goes into town to see her family, but she knows there are these emergencies and…'

Alice checked the temperature of the water in the bath, ran in a little more hot. 'I'll babysit,' she offered. 'I think Fiona and I can be friends now and I am a nurse. So I'll finish bathing her, put her to bed and read her a story. You and Mrs McCann can both go out.'

'I can't ask you to do that! You are a guest here.'

'You're not asking. I'm volunteering. Now, just sit here and splash water over your daughter while I go and change out of this dress.'

'But, Alice—'

'Ben! You know very well that for all concerned it's the obvious thing to do.'

He looked at her a moment. 'You always were decisive, weren't you? You made up your mind what had to be done and then you did it, even though it hurt.'

She wondered what he was referring to. Their parting perhaps? But now wasn't the time to go over old times. She just said, 'I'll be right back down.'

It didn't take long to organise things with him and Mrs McCann. Ben went out first then Mrs McCann showed Alice all that she needed to know. The housekeeper was quietly but obviously pleased that she could go out—even though she was more than willing to stay if she was needed.

So in fifteen minutes Alice had the house and Fiona to herself. She didn't regret offering to babysit, this was how the islanders were. They helped each other. But she wondered later what she would have thought as an eighteen-year-old if she could have seen the future. Yes, she could—she had—imagined the future, sitting reading a bedtime story to Ben's daughter. But she would have been the mother.

CHAPTER THREE

'I'M A happy man now,' Ben said. 'There's nothing I need. I love the island, I love my work. And most of all I've got my daughter and I love her most and there's no way I can lose her. My life's centred on her, like I said, I'm a happy man.'

'You're lucky,' Alice said with feeling. 'Being happy isn't easy. But a single man with a child? Does everyone on the island know that you're divorced?'

Suddenly his face was grim and Alice wished she hadn't asked. 'Everyone does know. But no one really knows why. No reason why they should, it's my affair. Still, what they don't know they make up. You know that's the way people are here, they're interested. But the other side is that there's always help if you need it.'

Alice grinned. 'Remember the two of us going on a cycle ride down to Brochel Point? It started to rain. We knew it would be over quite soon so we sheltered in that old barn.'

He sighed. 'I do remember! It got sunny again after fifteen minutes so we were able to carry on.'

'And both sets of parents knew that we'd been in the barn together before we even got home.'

He nodded. 'There's no keeping a secret here.'

'But it's nice to know that you belong.'

Somehow the conversation seemed to have veered from being about Ben's divorce. There was still a lot more Alice wanted to know about Ben's wife. And wasn't she entitled to? After all, so many years ago she had vaguely thought that she would be his wife. Still, that wasn't something that she could really say.

It was later in the evening. Ben had come back from seeing his patient, gone in to see his sleeping daughter, stared at her a while and then kissed her. He agreed with Alice that Fiona had some kind of not too serious infection. Then they had eaten in the kitchen, a casserole that Mrs McCann had left in the oven. And now they were sitting relaxed in the living room.

Alice was sitting with her back to the end of a leather couch, her legs stretched out along it, her shoes on the floor. Ben was sprawled in a matching easy chair, with his feet on a pouffe. In the corner a child alarm recorded the grunts and murmurs from the sleeping Fiona.

It was nearly dark but the curtains were undrawn. And through the window there was a view of the sun setting crimson into the now grey sea. It was so beautiful, Alice thought. Was there a view in London to compare with this? For the moment she felt happy, at peace with the world.

Ben walked over to her, filled her glass with more white wine. 'My marriage was a disaster,' he said as he moved back to his chair, 'but you don't want to hear about that.'

In fact, Alice very much wanted to hear about it but she thought it probably wasn't a good idea to say so right now. So she merely said, 'I'd like to know if you want to tell me some time. But it can't be too much of a disaster since you've got Fiona.'

Ben smiled. 'True. I have my daughter, Fiona Alice Cavendish, the best thing in my life.'

I wonder if he ever thought that I was the best thing in his life, Alice asked herself but obviously she said nothing. Instead, 'Fiona *Alice* Cavendish? Why Alice?'

His voice was calm. 'I always liked the name.'

Alice felt miffed. She'd given him the chance of saying something nice about her. Perhaps just something about the memory of happy youthful days with her—and he had ignored it. However…

Then there was silence, a grim silence, and Alice regretted asking him about the divorce. After a moment she gently said, 'Ben, I don't like seeing you like this. I don't remember you as an angry person.'

He sighed. 'I don't want to lumber you with my troubles. But I want to make a point to you. I'm telling you so you won't expect me to be the old Ben. I'm a different man, Alice. I'm harder, not the adolescent I was fifteen years ago. Perhaps I've grown up. I don't trust people the way I used to. I especially don't trust women who talk about love.'

He stood, walked towards her. 'Your glass is empty. Let me fill it.'

Alice blinked, she hadn't even noticed herself drinking.

The two of them sat quietly for a while. Ben apparently was calming down but Alice found herself getting more angry. This was the man she once had—years ago—hoped to marry. His child should have been hers. She wondered further. Ben seemed to have made as big a mess of his life as she had of hers.

It was Ben who first voiced what they were both obviously thinking. 'Who would have thought all that time ago that we would finish up like this?'

Alice felt the urge to be a little more positive. 'We've both got the careers we wanted. We're both happy in our work—well, I am and I think you are. You're obviously very happy with Fiona. But…' Her voice trailed away.

He had always listened carefully. 'But what?' he asked.

'Just but.' She didn't know what to say and he now had that alert look that she remembered so well. What could she say? And then she was saved as the baby alarm sputtered into life. Fiona was crying.

Ben jumped to his feet. Alice said, 'Ben, let me go. I can tell that cry, she's not going to go back to sleep easily. You've had a hard day, you look worn out. And I've had things easy.'

'But you're a guest here.'

'Ben! Let's get one thing straight. We've both got specialities and this one is mine. In this I'm more experienced than you, I've nursed hundreds of children who are in this state. I'm better at this than you are, Ben, and I expect you to recognise it.'

He shook his head and smiled. 'What did I say to you earlier about you used to be decisive? I understated the case. Yes, I am tired. And if you can get my little girl off to sleep, that would be wonderful.'

Alice nodded and left.

It wasn't easy getting Fiona to sleep again. She was hot so Alice sponged her down gently, then put her in fresh pyjamas. Still no sign of sleep—so of all things Alice tried singing to her. She had done this before. Not a good idea if you had more than one child in a ward—but if you were one to one sometimes it worked well. She sang a couple of lullabies that had been sung in the islands for years. And Fiona slept.

Ben crept quietly into the bedroom when Fiona was nearly asleep. Alice put her finger to her lips, waved at him to be silent and to sit on the single bed in the corner of the room. And soon Fiona was asleep.

Alice went to sit by Ben. 'She's going to have a bad night,' she said. 'She's going to wake often, probably be sick again. She's going to need attention so I think I ought to sleep the night in this bed to be near her.'

'I can't ask you to do that!'

'You didn't ask. I offered. Ben, you know it makes sense. You've got to work tomorrow, I don't. I suspect this fever will be over by then, Fiona will be quiet and sleep most of the day. If I want, I can sleep through the day as well.'

'But I'm her father! You're a guest.'

'You've said that already. Looking after Fiona will make me feel that I'm earning my keep. Besides, I want to look after her.'

Ben looked at her speculatively for a moment. 'Thank you,' he said. 'I'll accept your offer.'

He went over and looked down at his sleeping child. Alice wondered at his expression and then she remembered. Once he'd looked at her the same way.

Not exactly the same, but similar. And always when he'd thought she wasn't looking at him. As if everything he could want in life was there. Alice shrugged, angrily. She must be tired too, having foolish thoughts like these!

They decided that Fiona could be left alone a little longer and went down to the now dark living room. For some reason they didn't turn on the lights, but sat there with only the light of the moon reflected off the sea. Alice was pleased that all she could see of Ben was the vague shadow of his body. She didn't want to have to look at his face, she thought she could read too much in it. And who knew if she was reading right?

Ben seemed to sense her mood, to realise that knowing he had been married and was now divorced had disturbed her. After a while he said, 'I've no right to feel disappointed with my life. I've made a bit of a mess of things— but I've got my work and I've got Fiona. That's more than a lot of people have. Perhaps I should be grateful.'

Alice liked him for what he had just said, but she felt a bit left out of things. So the only reply she could make was, 'Perhaps you should.'

Ben seemed to hear the implicit criticism in her voice. He asked, 'Who or what have you got that is important, Alice? What is dearest to you?'

'I've got this job that I'm very much looking forward to. In a year's time I've been promised a job in London. I've got my career and that is enough.'

'But you have nobody special?'

'You mean have I got a man in tow? No, I have nobody. Like you've I've tried it and it didn't work. So being without is the way I like it, being alone saves trouble and energy.'

'That seems a bit extreme. How did you—?'

Alice sighed quietly to herself. She was tired, she didn't want this conversation. The last thing she needed was to share her feelings with a man who had just told her that he didn't trust people the way he used to. Why had he picked that word 'trust'? It meant so much to her.

She was saved by Fiona again. There was another wail from the baby alarm. She said, 'Why don't you go up to her bedroom and stroke her head for a while? I'll go to my room, get ready for bed and come there in twenty minutes. I noticed that the bed was made up so I can get straight in.'

'Right,' he said.

Alice went to her room, had the swiftest of showers. Now, what to wear? She only had a small selection of clothes with her, all she had to sleep in was a long T-shirt with the words 'Cuddle me, I've had a hard day' printed on the front. It would have to do. She put it on, wrapped her dressing-gown around her. Not the woollen one she would wear in winter but a light silk gown. She had been expecting to sleep in her own bedroom or a hotel. This gown clung to her, she felt just a touch exposed as she walked down the corridor.

Ben had got Fiona nearly to sleep. He looked at Alice, she thought she saw a flash of something in those wonderful grey eyes—but it was dark in the room. Perhaps she had been mistaken.

He said, 'My room is right next door. If there's any problem—'

'Ben, I've told you I'm fine. Now, switch off the baby alarm and go to sleep.'

One long last look at her and he was gone.

Alice went over to look at the sleeping Fiona and shook her head. This is not the way I had anticipated looking after Ben Cavendish's child, she thought. Then she went and slid into her bed.

There was one last thought. Why had Ben been so keen to offer her an explanation of his past? To tell her that he wasn't the old Ben, but a much harder version who would never trust a woman again? Was he trying to warn her against something? Or perhaps trying to strengthen his own resolve? Perhaps there were memories of feelings for her that he wanted to repress before they came back. Now, that was an interesting thought.

And what about her feelings for him? Well, there were feelings—but she didn't want to think about them too closely. He was still a very attractive man.

Time she went to sleep.

CHAPTER FOUR

SHE was woken up three times in the night but she had learned the nurse's trick of going straight back to sleep when it was needed. Fiona was at her worst at three in the morning—but after the last ten minutes of crying, it was obvious to the trained eye and ear that she was improving.

She was a little put out however when she had to be gently woken by Mrs McCann—cup of tea in hand. 'How's the bairn?' she whispered.

Alice blinked weary eyes, swung her legs out of bed and reached for her dressing-gown. She padded over, felt Fiona's forehead. 'Getting better,' she said. 'Fever is definitely down. Today she'll be a lot better. We'll let her sleep as long as she wants.'

'Dr Cavendish says would you like to go back to your own room and stay in bed a while? I'll look after Fiona for the rest of the day.'

Alice shook her head. 'No. I'm a nurse, I'm used to getting up in the night. I'd best get up now. Besides, I'm here to work, not sleep.'

Mrs McCann looked at her thoughtfully. 'I thought you were a guest. But I prefer someone who will work.'

You'd not find that kind of comment from a house-keeper in London, Alice thought with a secret grin.

Mrs McCann went on, 'I'll serve you breakfast in twenty minutes with the doctor.' Then she tiptoed over to look at the sleeping Fiona and was gone.

Alice went back to her own room, quickly showered and dressed. Today a dark linen trouser suit, she wanted to look slightly formal. And as she dressed she thought about the last twenty-four hours. She felt a bit…not un-comfortable but unsure of what she was doing. Whatever she had expected, it had not been this. She had been thrown into Ben's family life and she wasn't sure it was good for her. Of course, it was good to see some-thing of Ben, and she really liked Fiona. But she needed to take charge of her own life again.

She went back to have a quick look at the still sleeping Fiona, and while she was rearranging the bed-clothes there was the gentlest of taps on the door. It was Ben, dressed in dark trousers, white shirt but with no tie.

Alice felt a sudden tightness in her chest. There was the shock of recognition, a brief remembrance of feelings now fifteen years old. There was also the recognition that Ben was now different—but still a very attractive man. She thought she would have to be careful. She had just got over being betrayed by a very attractive man. Got over?

She sniffed. Stupid thoughts so early in the morning!

'Are you sure you're all right, getting up?' Ben asked after he too had been to peer at his daughter. 'Mrs McCann said you were determined to.'

'I am. I'm fine. And Fiona seems a bit better to me. She'll be all right in Mrs McCann's care today.'

With the most tender of fingers Ben stroked a curl from Fiona's forehead. 'Did you have a disturbed night?'

Good, they were playing doctor and nurse, not Ben and Alice. Right now this was the way she wanted it. 'Not too bad. She woke up three times. I got her back to sleep quite quickly each time.'

'Quite quickly?' he asked with a small smile, and she realised that he didn't quite believe her.

'Nothing I couldn't cope with. I feel fine now.'

There was silence for a moment as he studied her and then he said, 'Breakfast is ready when you are. Are you sure that you wouldn't like to take it easy?'

She shook her head. 'I didn't come here to take things easy. I came here to work. Are you going to the surgery this morning?'

He nodded. 'Just as usual.'

'Could you take me into town? Drop me off at the clinic where I'm supposed to work? I know I'm early but I'd like to look around.'

'I think that's a good idea,' he said.

It was what she wanted. Or what she needed, which was different. She felt that her life since her return had been too wrapped up in Ben and his family. It had happened by accident. But now she needed distance, needed time to remember who she was.

Yesterday, on the drive out of town, she had been too shocked at meeting Ben to pay too much attention to her surroundings. Now, as they drove back, there was time to look around. First, a careful study of the hills that backed the town. All the locals did this first thing in the morning as the hills tended to reflect what the weather was going to be. And today the weather was going to be fine.

Once again, memories came crowding back, she couldn't help herself. She had to talk to him, to share. 'Look, that's where I had a puncture in my bike tyre. On our first trip out to see the house. We hadn't known each other very long—well, not that well. You showed me how to mend the puncture, putting the inner tube in that stream so the bubbles would show where the hole was.'

She was silent a while and then said, 'You never see people mending punctures in London. Well, not by the roadside. I suppose they must have them.'

'I suppose so. I think I remember the puncture,' he said shortly.

But now she remembered more than the flat tyre. 'It was warm. When it was mended we sat in the sun for a while.'

Then she decided not to say any more. They had done a little more than just sit in the sun. He had kissed her once or twice already. But then he had…and with her definite compliance… It had been only a childish fumble but it had been exciting and frightening and so good. A different age! In London she had dealt with girls of that age who were now having their second child.

Glancing sideways at him, she saw the set face. Obviously he remembered too. But he wasn't going to remember it with the same joy as she did. Why not? After a while he said, 'They were good times, but we were young then. We have more sense now.'

'It would be nice to think so,' she said.

Then there was silence as they drove the rest of the way into town.

On the outskirts of town they passed a large old house that had been home to Ben and his father. A surgery had been built onto the side of it. But now the house had been extended even further, the garden had been converted into a car park and there was a sign that said 'Mountain View Hotel'.

'Your old house is a hotel?' Alice queried.

Ben laughed. 'We have to move with the times. You'll find the new surgery much more convenient.' And, ten minutes later, she did.

They drove into the forecourt of a set of buildings that were obviously new, but faced with the local grey stone. Alice looked on approvingly. 'Welcome to Soalay Medical Centre,' Ben said. 'That entrance is to my little kingdom—the surgery. Over there is your entrance and your part. There's the clinic, and next to it your new birthing unit, with your flat built over the top. So we're together but separate. We even have separate receptionists—though you will share yours with the district nurse.'

'Together but separate,' she echoed. 'Right.' She wondered if he was talking about their relationship as well as their places of work. She didn't know.

'I'll take you in and introduce you to Morag Watson, she's the district nurse here. She'll show you around. Then I'll leave you with her because I've got morning surgery. Meet for a coffee at lunchtime?'

'I certainly won't need any lunch after that breakfast,' she said.

* * *

Ben had a ritual at work. He arrived early, said hello to his receptionist and picked up any messages. Then he sat alone in his room, drank a large coffee, read his mail and thought about the day ahead. Although he was always busy he gave himself just fifteen minutes—and usually found it fifteen minutes well spent. And today he had more to think about than usual.

He had to think about Alice. When he had first seen her yesterday, windblown on the deck of the ferry, he had been amazed at how memories of the past had come hurtling back. He had not seen her for fifteen years, she had slowly passed out of his memory. His life had been full, he'd had other things to think about. But suddenly it had all come back. He remembered her as a schoolgirl and him as a schoolboy. They had worked together on their science homework. They had quartered the island on their bikes. And then he remembered their youthful fumblings. A voyage of exploration that now came back to life with a force that was almost painful. A kiss then had been so sweet! When she had talked about mending the puncture he had known that the puncture had not been the thing uppermost in her mind. That had been the first occasion he had slid his hand under her shirt and… What would that be like now? He mustn't think that way!

He drank his coffee, tried to calm himself. Alice was different now. He could still see the schoolgirl she had been, but she had changed. Some of the gawkiness had gone, her curves had matured, she was now a woman, not a girl. He suspected that the haircut that looked so simple and artless was quite expensive. It was quite different from the close crop she'd had when younger. Her face too had changed. He suspected there was sadness there—or perhaps just experience. Then it struck him. Her face had always been attractive—perhaps in an unformed way—but now she was classically beautiful.

Today was unusual. Every morning he had a cup of coffee and it lasted the fifteen minutes he needed as his thinking time. But now the coffee-cup was empty and he needed another—after just five minutes. Things were bad.

He fetched himself another coffee and sat at his desk again. He just wasn't facing up to the present situation. He had been instantly attracted to Alice when he had seen her again. But was this just a hangover from the feelings of his youth? And another thing. He was divorced. Getting divorced had hurt, he had tried, really tried, because he thought that marriages should last. So now he was wary, the last thing he needed was another love affair. He remembered the expression—'on the rebound'. Well, he was a man, not a tennis ball.

Then he had to smile. For a moment he had been thinking that all he had to do was decide himself what happened between he and Alice. But what were her thoughts? She'd made them very clear. The last thing she needed was a man. She felt exactly the same as he did. There was no problem.

Alice had intended to look around her new premises, perhaps look at her flat and see how it was getting on. She wanted to ease herself into her new job. She thought she needed a bit of time alone to see what she was about to do. But she wasn't to be alone. The person with whom she would share the new premises was already there. Ben made the briefest introductions and then left.

There was no problem. Alice knew at once that she was going to get on with Morag Watson, the district nurse.

Morag was in her fifties and in spite of having spent eight years on Soalay had lost none of her Glasgow accent. 'Born in Glasgow, trained in Glasgow, worked in Glasgow,' she told Alice. 'Then I thought I'd come to the islands and take things easy for a while. Easy? It would have been easier joining the Scots Guards.'

She hustled through the set of her own well-appointed rooms, showing Alice where everything was kept. 'Now, I'm hoping there's going to be no territorial problems with medicines and dressings and rooms and things like that. I want to use anything of yours that I haven't got and I'm expecting that you'll make free with what is technically my—'

There was banging that appeared to come from the front door. 'I suspect we're in business,' Morag said as they hastened to open it. 'Come on, you might be able to help.'

'But I can't help. I'm not insured yet and—'

'Are you going to tell that to that child who is wailing outside?'

At the front door was a tearful, white-faced mother, obviously shocked, clutching an even more tearful child. 'I know you're not open yet,' she sobbed as Morag opened the door, 'but…'

Morag pulled the woman inside. 'Take the child,' she said to Alice.

The woman went on, 'Angus there pulled at the kettle

when I was not looking. I jumped to grab him but he spilt boiling water all over his chest and my hands.'

'We can see to it,' Morag said. 'Now, come through and sit down in the clinic. Alice, can you deal with Angus there?'

'I'm fine,' said Alice, reaching for the child. Morag was right. There was no way she could worry about insurance when there was a child in pain and she had the means to deal with that pain.

'You're Mrs Allan, aren't you?' Morag was saying. 'Eileen Allan? I've seen you in the clinic here. Tell me, Eileen, what did you do when you first got scalded? Did you put any ointment or anything like that on the burns?'

'No. I saw this programme on television, it said just put the hurt bit under cold running water. So I did that.'

'How long for?'

Eileen looked confused. 'Just for a minute. Till my hands felt cold and Angus's chest seemed cold too.'

'If it ever happens again, leave them there longer,' Morag said. 'Now, sit down here, don't worry about things, you're both going to be all right. And here's a blanket to wrap round you, we don't want you getting cold.'

She turned to Alice. 'There's a gown hanging in that cupboard, it should fit you. Gloves and the burns kit are here. Everything OK?'

'No problem. I've done this before.' Alice knew that she could cope—easily. She hadn't expected to start work today, but she could. She fetched the gown and gloves.

'Everything's going to be all right,' she said to Angus, 'I know it hurts now but we can soon make that hurt go away.' It was important to try to soothe Angus, make sure he wasn't afraid that things were going to get worse.

'Is he going to be all right?' Eileen's tearful voice came from behind her. 'Is my baby badly hurt?'

At the sound of his mother's anxious voice, Angus started to cry more than ever.

'Nurse Muir will look after Angus and do a good job,' Alice heard Morag say, quite sharply. 'Now, stop worrying about him and let me look at these hands. Did you know that when I started nursing, the doctor told me to put honey on burns?'

'Honey?' asked a startled Eileen, 'Why on earth use honey?' Alice grinned. Morag knew how to divert someone who was interfering with a situation.

Quickly she checked Angus's little body but the only injury was to the chest. She diagnosed the scald as superficial and partial—partial because the total area injured was less than the area of his hand. The skin was red and moist, it looked granular. And it hurt—which was a good thing. A burn that didn't hurt was serious. The nerves were deadened.

In the burns kit there was paediatric paracetamol syrup, Alice gave him a dose and then made a note of what she had done. She covered the burn with the rec-ommended powder and then a loose dressing. The skin was the natural barrier against infection in the body. Far too many burns resulted in a more serious infection.

'There you are, Angus,' she said, tucking a blanket round him. 'Just lie there and sleep if you can. We're going to keep you here for a while and then you can go home with your mummy and everything will be all right.'

She looked up, saw Morag silently pointing at a drawer. Alice opened the drawer and grinned—there was a set of tiny teddy-bear badges, each teddy bear with a bandaged arm and leg. She took a badge. 'And this is for you for being brave,' she said.

Angus looked down proudly as she pinned the badge to his coat.

'Angus is fine now,' Alice said to Morag and Eileen. 'The burns should have healed in ten or twenty days.'

'So we'll all celebrate,' said Morag. 'Three cups of tea and an orange juice.'

Just before lunchtime there was a call for Alice from Ben's receptionist. Ben would have to work through his lunch-break so there would be no time for coffee. Could she stay with Morag? And there had been a phone call from Mrs McCann. Fiona was quiet but doing fine.

'There's always work here if you look for it,' Morag said. 'Especially for Dr Cav. He seems to go out of his way to look for work so I'm hoping you'll make his life easier. Anyway, enough of medicine—come and look at your flat. It's still like a building site but you can get some idea.'

Well, it had been a building site but now it was nearly finished. Alice thought it was wonderful—compared with the nurses' accommodation in London it was a palace. It was in an extension of the main building, on the first floor above her new birthing unit. She had her own living room, kitchen and bathroom. There was a big bedroom and a smaller one that could be used as a study. The furniture seemed to be tasteful but unfortunately it was piled up in the centre of the living room and covered with a large white sheet. A decorator was working industriously, painting the living-room walls a pleasant shade of yellow.

'Be about another week before we're finished, ladies,' he said. 'There's a bit of plumbing to sort out and then the carpets to fit.'

'I'll be watching you, Henry Chappel,' Morag threatened. 'Make sure you do a good job.'

'Don't I always?' The painter winked at Alice.

'You're not bad,' Morag allowed. 'But we'll be in every day to see how you're getting on.' When they had gone downstairs she asked Alice, 'What do you think of the place?'

'I think it's wonderful. And who chose the furniture? It's just right.'

'Dr Cav chose it. Said he'd seen too many medical buildings ruined by letting a committee choose stuff. Now, let's go and look at your birthing unit.'

Alice had already seen the specifications of the unit, but it was different to see it already built. Her very own MLU—midwifery-led unit. There were two delivery rooms, an assessment room, a larger room to be used as a clinic. There was an ultrasound scanner— she had gone on a year-long course to be trained to use the machine.

'You're going to be your own boss in here,' Morag commented. 'Your new mums will be perfectly happy here, they'll have individual one-to-one care. I bet once people hear about this place that the town birth rate will go up.'

'I'm not sure that's the purpose of the exercise,' Alice said.

But she was very happy with the place. It fell in line with her own ideas about child-bearing—that the more personal the attention was, the happier the mother would be. Of course, she could only deal with comparatively simple cases. Anyone needing a Caesarean, for example, would have to be shipped to a hospital on the mainland. But most cases were simple and Alice could cope. In fact, there would usually be no need to involve a doctor at all. She was a registered midwife practitioner and so could prescribe the drugs she thought necessary.

Morag led her outside. 'And last of all—your own private ambulance. Though you'll use it most for your usual calls.' It was a long-wheelbase Land Rover, fitted with a bunk and a special carrier for a newborn.

Alice inspected it, open-mouthed. 'I never expected anything like this!'

Morag nodded happily. 'Good, isn't it? Dr Cav fought for it. Said he didn't want to have to order any more helicopters from the mainland for medical emergencies. Said that this would be safer—and cheaper too in the long run. That man can be convincing when he puts his mind to it. Ever driven anything like this before?'

'Never. I'm more used to driving an old van at fifteen miles an hour through the streets of London. I even thought I might have to turn into an old-fashioned midwife and travel everywhere by bike.'

'Those times are gone,' Morag said half sadly. 'Are you going to be happy here?'

'Very. I can't wait to move in and get started.'

They walked back to Morag's clinic. 'So d'you fancy working this afternoon? I've been having to cover a lot of the midwife's work and my own work has suffered a bit. There's three pregnancy examinations you could do.'

'I'd love to,' Alice said, and then hesitated. 'There's just one thing. I need to know that I'm insured. That it's all right for me to work. I've got to be covered. I'm not supposed to start for a week.'

Morag looked at her curiously. 'I'm not asking you to do anything drastic,' she said. 'No deliveries or anything. Just simple examinations.'

'I'd still like you to phone Ben to make sure it's OK.'

Alice could see that Morag was a bit surprised by this, even a little hurt. Then she looked at Alice shrewdly. 'You've got a reason for asking, haven't you? A definite reason, something that happened not too long ago?'

Clever of her. Alice thought. But she merely said, 'I've learned that it's always best to be covered. Tell you what, let me phone Ben and explain. He can phone the trust and get things sorted out.'

She didn't like bothering him but it was something she felt needed to be done. When she got through it was obvious that Ben didn't think there was a problem either. But he said he'd ask his receptionist to get in touch with the trust and ask their opinion. And fifteen minutes later he phoned back. 'You're covered. Have a good afternoon. What do you think of your new home?'

'Ben, it's wonderful! I couldn't have designed anything better myself.'

'I'm glad you're pleased. I spent a lot of time working on the plans. Now, you're coming back with me to stay tonight?'

She hesitated…but it was the obvious thing to do. 'If you'll have me,' she said, 'I'd love to.'

She found that she was looking forward to going home with him. Then she frowned. Why was she looking forward to it?

Fiona was still very tired but much better. When Alice and Ben got back to Taighean dhe Gaoithe she had been bathed and fed by Mrs McCann but allowed to stay up until she had seen Ben. He put her to bed while Alice sat in the living room and stared out to sea.

She wondered quite what she was doing there. Why was she feeling so comfortable, so much at home? She had come here to be mistress of her own fate, to have her own place to live, her own place to work. To be beholden to no one. And she'd promptly found herself living in the house of an ex-boyfriend. It wasn't a good idea.

A week until her flat was finished? Well, she supposed she could manage that. And then, when she'd moved in, perhaps she'd have a better perspective on things. Life at the moment seemed…odd.

However, a couple of hours later she was feeling slightly different. After a wonderful meal cooked by Mrs McCann (fish landed not three hours before) she was sitting with Ben again and staring happily out at the setting sun. 'It's been sunny every day I've spent so far in Soalay,' she said. 'All two of them.'

Ben laughed. 'Don't get carried away by that idea. You must remember the weather here. It can turn from sun to rain in the time it takes you to open your umbrella.'

'I remember. I've packed my waterproofs.'

They sat there for a while longer in companionable silence. In the background were grumblings from Fiona's baby alarm.

'We both agree that she will probably sleep through tonight,' Ben said, 'so you can sleep in your own bed and I'll have the alarm in my room as before. There should be no—'

'She still might wake up,' Alice said, 'so I'd quite like to sleep in her bedroom again. Just in case. And if she does wake up a lot, I could do as you suggested and sleep in tomorrow morning.'

Ben looked at her and laughed. 'You stay in bed tomorrow morning? Do you expect me to believe that?'

Alice sighed. 'Perhaps not. But, Ben, I do want to sleep in her room tonight.'

She could tell he was thinking, she had forgotten just how shrewd he could be. 'There are reasons you want to sleep in Fiona's room?' he asked quietly. 'Special reasons?'

She didn't answer for a moment. Then, 'Yes, there are reasons. But I don't want to go into them now. If it's all right with you.'

'It's all right. And if you're sure you don't mind… I'm very happy for you to sleep there with her. I can't think of anyone I'd rather have as her nurse.'

Alice felt warm at this. So he appreciated her. As a nurse.

They both gazed out at the setting sun again. After a while he said, 'I only found out about a week ago that it was you who would be coming here. It gave me quite a shock. Our usual midwife-cum-children's nurse has taken a year's maternity leave and decided to stay with her husband's family on the mainland. She said she knew that if she stayed here she'd still work—so it was better to leave. I have to agree with her. Anyway, the trust contracted with an agency to find a replacement, they found a Miss Prendergast. She was very well quali-fied but she'd spent most of her life working in a town-centre hospital. She was nearly sixty. I liked her but I didn't think she was quite the ideal for a place where you need to be out and about all the time. Still, we needed someone desperately and I thought we could make things work. Then I got a message saying that Miss Prendergast had dropped out and that you were coming in her place. What happened to her, do you know?'

Alice had to giggle. 'Sorry, it's not really funny,' she said. 'But just a week ago Miss Prendergast was out walking her dog, tripped over the lead and fell and broke her leg. And I'd just signed on with the agency, offering them a year's work anywhere. Anywhere as far from London as possible. And they offered me this position.'

'Why was it important to be as far from London as possible?'

She wasn't yet ready to explain it all to him. So she just shrugged. 'I'd been there fifteen years. I needed a rest.'

She suspected that he didn't entirely believe her. He had always been astute, always able to guess at her feelings. Still, it was a reasonable story.

'So it was a complete coincidence that you came back to Soalay?'

'Yes, it was a complete coincidence. And I didn't know you'd be here until I'd signed the contract.' She knew that he'd believe that. After all it was entirely true. 'But I did wonder...can you ever come back to a place when you've left it apparently for good?'

'So have you happy memories of here or not?'

Suddenly they were on dangerous ground. This was a question that could lead to trouble, lead to things being aired that they had both carefully tried to disregard. The peaceful atmosphere that had been in the room suddenly seemed charged with electricity.

She looked across at him, apparently at ease in his seat. He looked as casual as ever but she sensed that a lot would depend on her answer. But she had always tried to be direct. She had to be the same now.

'Most of my memories are to do with you,' she said. 'And they are...happy memories.'

'We were very close. And I...'

Then she sensed that he felt that he had to back away from anything that might be seen as a statement. An endorsement of the feelings that she knew he had then.

'But we were children,' he went on. 'We didn't know what we were doing, what feelings were, we didn't know how the world worked. We had to get away into the wide world.'

'It did us both good?' she suggested. 'It was something that we had to do?'

'Perhaps.'

Then he said something that astonished her. 'I felt

that I talked you into going to London—into our parting. I did think it would be good for you. But I always hoped you'd change your mind. I wanted you to come to Edinburgh with me, as we'd agreed. But once you had decided, that was it. I had to respect that.'

It was a shock. She had never known he'd felt that way! She didn't know what to say, she didn't know what she wanted to say. After a while she muttered, 'I enjoyed the London course, I felt I learned a lot. Things could have been different but I…'

Her voice trailed away. What was the use of talking? She said, 'I think I'm tired, I'll go to bed now.'

His voice was soft. 'Goodnight Alice. You know you don't have to stay with Fiona, don't you? I feel I'm putting on you.'

'I want to stay with her.'

Perhaps she was more tired than she'd thought or perhaps because he had just shocked her by telling her how he had wanted her to stay with him. Was it a good time to share confidences? She just didn't know. She had walked as far as the door before she made up her mind. Then she turned, walked back and sat down again.

'I want to tell you one thing, just tell one simple thing. I don't want any long explanation or discussion. I just want you to listen. Like a doctor and a patient. But I don't want any medicine or suggested cure. I just want to tell you facts.'

'I can listen.' He was obviously intrigued.

'About six months ago I had a miscarriage at twenty weeks. Just old enough to kick me, to let me know that he or she was there. It was a wanted baby—well, I wanted it. In my time I've counselled lots of women about this. Telling them that things like this just happen. One out of every five conceptions results in a miscarriage. Often it's nature's way of telling you that this birth is not a good idea. I used to come out with all these platitudes and I believed in them. But when it happened to me I realised that I didn't know what I was talking about. It hurts and it makes you afraid. So can you now understand why I want to stay with Fiona. She's a lovely little girl.'

'I hope she can help you,' Ben said. 'And, Alice, I'm so sorry for you.'

CHAPTER FIVE

IT WAS only her flat that wasn't complete. Her birthing unit was ready for use and after Ben had stepped in she was insured to practise. She was also insured to drive her Land Rover. When she was dropped off the next day she found more parcels had arrived, including a set of uniforms.

She spent the morning checking her stock, familiar-ising herself with everything, putting things in their proper place. Whoever had done the ordering had done a good job. She wondered if it was the broken-legged Miss Prendergast—or could it have been Ben? For some reason she thought that more likely. When she had finished her morning's work she went to see Morag, who had been doubling up as district nurse and midwife. She asked to see if there were any current files, any work that she could take over.

Morag handed her three files. 'These three mothers-to-be live far out of town and for various reasons they find it hard to get in for a check-up. It wouldn't be a bad idea if two had mid term visits and one is further advanced than that—she should have phoned in for an appointment but she hasn't. I just haven't had a chance to get out to see any of them. If you fancy driving round in your new vehicle, it'd be a good idea to pay them all a visit.'

'Great,' said Alice. She checked her midwife's bag, worked out a route from the map and gingerly set off. The three visits were at the far end of the island but reasonably close together.

Driving the Land Rover was very different from driving the little car she had sold before she'd left London. It seemed vast. It seemed high. But she knew that she would soon come to love it. And there was so little traffic. She was more likely to see tractors than lumbering red buses. She was loving this. She could smell real air instead of traffic fumes and the views were stupendous.

As she drove along the narrow country lanes she felt like a real midwife. A feeling she'd not had for a while. After the chaos and misery of the past few weeks this was a real treat. She had given in her notice after the hearing and reprimand but had managed to leave at once because she was owed some holiday time.

But now she was happy. She used to cycle round here with Ben then told herself to forget that. She had to live in the present, not the past. One other thing was nice— a lot of the people in the rare passing traffic waved at her. Well, she was obviously a nurse or something medical. The blue and white paintwork suggested that, as well as the name on the side. She was enjoying herself.

Cara Garrett lived in a tiny croft in the even tinier hamlet of Lonkille. This was the flatter edge of the island and Alice had to skirt a long stretch of boggy land before she reached Lonkille. It was just a handful of grey cottages scattered around a bay at the far north of the island. The road to get there was wild and lonely but it was another lovely day and the drive was beautiful.

Alice stopped before she got to the cottage and reread Cara's notes. Cara already had a son, two-year-old Hamish, and she was now twenty-six weeks pregnant. The twenty-week assessment had been fine. Pencilled notes said that the husband was a fisherman often away for long periods but that the neighbours were reliable and could be called on. These weren't official notes. Pencil was easy to erase.

It was a good visit. Cara made tea and then wanted to chat about how Alice had once been an islander. Hamish was playing in the garden, Alice had a look at him and found him to be a bright toddler. No problems whatsoever with this family. Alice talked a while about where Cara was to have the baby and found that she wanted to come to the birthing unit. That was good. Well, it was safer and it made for less work.

The second visit was just as straightforward. The mother-to-be really wanted to deliver in the clinic. No problems here either. A chat and they parted friends.

Alice was beginning to think that all her work on the island would be straightforward. She should have known better. The third visit was not so good.

Her suspicions started when she saw that the white-washed cottage had a great garish rainbow painted on one side. It didn't look well against the cool greens and greys of the landscape. To one side of the cottage was a rickety-looking windmill. There was a reasonable breeze blowing, but the sails weren't turning. Alice started to wonder.

When she got closer she saw that there had been an unsuccessful attempt at making a kitchen garden. The vegetables planted just weren't right for this soil and this climate. There were dogs playing outside and she saw thin goats in a paddock at the back.

Alice sighed. There had been quite a few incomers to the island when she had been at school. If they didn't already know, most of them quickly found out what living on a northern island was like. Often they had to change their preconceived ideas. And the successful ones stayed because they loved the place and they were made welcome. They learned to adapt to the climate, to the occasional harshness of the life. But those who had their own ideas about living the simple life, who refused to recognise how hard things could be, well, usually they didn't last long. Still, it wasn't her place to judge and she hoped this family would be happy.

She was here to look at thirty-two week pregnant Debbie Laws, to ensure that Debbie had good prospects for a safe birth and that her baby had the best possible start in life.

Debbie looked washed-out, white-faced. Her hair needed both cutting and combing. She was wearing a long, semi-peasant-type dress and that didn't appear too clean. Her breasts looked full but she wore no bra. Must be uncomfortable, Alice thought.

Debbie didn't have much to say but seemed pleased to see Alice. She sat her at the table, made them both the obligatory cup of tea. Herbal tea, Alice found. It was…different. When she heard Debbie's accent, Alice had to smile. Debbie had spent most of her life in London.

'I'm glad you've come,' Debbie said. 'We don't get too many visitors.'

'Well, I've just been appointed midwife and children's nurse here and I'm trying to look at all the—'

'A midwife! Great, just what we need. Midwife, whatever your name is, I'm pleased to see you. Debbie's been a bit worried even though I've told her that there's nothing to worry about. So I need you to tell her I'm right. Let me introduce myself—I'm Freddie Laws.'

The door had banged open and there was a great bearded smiling man. He strode over to Debbie, put his arm round her smiled and kissed her in an obviously loving way. 'And this will be our first baby together. We hope to have more!'

'My name is Alice Muir,' Alice said. 'I'll be the midwife in charge.' Normally she wouldn't dream of using the words, 'in charge'. But she felt that it was necessary to establish a little authority. Debbie was a long way from her help and Freddie was a touch too confident.

Freddie's next words confirmed her suspicions. 'Giving birth is a natural process, not a medical emergency. Our child will be born at home. I'm not sure that we really need a midwife.'

'Giving birth at home is fine if you don't have an emergency,' Alice said. 'How many births have you supervised, Mr Laws?'

'None really. But men have been helping their wives

give birth for thousands of years. Of course, I'll appreciate your advice.'

'We've just had a new birthing unit installed at the clinic in Soalay,' Alice said. 'I'd like Debbie at least to look around it and—'

'She's having our baby at home,' Freddie said.

Alice decided that this was not the time to get into an argument. 'I'd like to have a look at you now,' she said, turning specifically to Debbie. 'According to the notes, at your last visit you seemed to be just a touch anaemic.'

'Anaemic? Rubbish! She was just a bit—'

Alice was wondering just what she'd have to say to make Freddie pay attention to her when they were interrupted by the loud ringing of a telephone. Freddie groped in his pocket, took out a mobile phone. 'Perry old friend, it's good to hear from you. And I'll bet I know what you want.'

Alice blinked. Freddie's voice had changed. Now he sounded like the complete city gent. He covered the mouthpiece of the phone, muttered, 'Excuse me, work calls,' and walked rapidly into another room, shutting the door behind him.

'That's always happening,' Debbie said.

'He works from here?'

'He's an accountant with a big firm in London, they email all his work up here. We used to live in Islington but Freddie said he wanted to get back to nature.'

'Right,' said Alice, 'I hope Freddie and nature are getting on fine. Now, is there a bedroom where I can have a look at you?'

Debbie's pregnancy was progressing quite satisfactorily. The previous midwife had prescribed iron tablets to try and deal with the slight anaemia—with the warning that drinking too much milk and taking iron tablets might bring on vomiting. Take vitamin C to aid the absorption of iron. Eat chocolate and as many green leafy vegetables as were available. Especially broccoli. The suggestions appeared to have worked well as there was now no sign of anaemia. Alice was satisfied—more or less. But there was another problem.

'I see you suffer from asthma,' she said to Debbie.

'I do. But I've been a lot better since I got here—ask Freddie. I think I'm cured.'

Asthma cured? Alice thought, but said nothing. 'Usually, if we have a patient with asthma, we like her to have her baby in hospital—in your case in my birthing centre. I'm very much in favour of home births and so far you seem to be doing very well. But there's always that tiniest chance—'

'But Freddie says—'

'Freddie is neither a doctor nor a midwife. But we'll see how things go over the next couple of weeks.' She wasn't tremendously happy about the prospect of Debbie having a baby at home—but decided not to say anything more on this visit. 'You're doing fine for now,' she said, 'but I'll be along to see you in a week or so. And don't forget! Any problems—ring me.'

'I'll do that,' said Debbie. 'Will you have another cup of tea before you go?' Alice winced but accepted.

They were drinking their tea when the door was pushed open and a young boy entered. Alice thought he looked pale, undernourished. He couldn't have been older than seven. 'This is Albert,' Debbie said. 'Say hello, Albert.'

'Hello,' Albert said listlessly. He came over to Alice and she held out her hand to him. Sometimes it was good to treat children as if they were adults. Albert reached for Alice's outstretched hand but missed it. 'I'm tired now,' he said after Alice had managed to grab his hand and shake it. He walked through the living room, slowly climbed the stairs against the far wall of the cottage and a moment later there was the slam of a door closing.

'He gets tired very easily,' Debbie said. 'He was all right when we came here but recently he's getting more and more tired. Spends a lot of time just lying on his bed.'

Alice frowned. 'I thought this was your first child?'

'Oh, it is, Albert is Freddie's child. There was this messy divorce—and I suppose I was a bit to blame. But Albert is with us now and we both love him.'

'You say he's been getting tired easily. I'd like the doctor to—'

'Albert is fine,' a voice boomed from behind her. 'There's nothing wrong with him that this fresh Scottish air won't cure. Midwife Muir, thanks for your concern but people rely too much on so-called medical science. There is no problem with Albert and I'll not have him hauled before a doctor. The great majority of people who go to see their GP need nothing more than rest. Albert is just needing time to fit into his new home.'

Freddie had come out of his study. And looking at his angry face Alice realised that he intended to have his own way. Unfortunately for him, she intended to have her own way—but she realised this wasn't the time to start a fight.

'Of course there's no problem,' she agreed. She knew that to win this fight she had to have reinforcements.

She'd enjoyed her visits but now there was paperwork to do. She spent the rest of the afternoon filling in forms, reviewing all the cases that she had been left, in general trying to get her new little empire ready so that she could concentrate most on the work that mattered—her patients. So far things had been quiet.

She left a message for Ben that she had finished all that she could usefully do for the day and would drive herself home. This was an evening when he had to work late. She had only been with Ben for two days—and yet she was thinking of his house as home. She would have to be careful. She and Ben were colleagues and friends—nothing more.

For a while she chatted to Mrs McCann and then she took Fiona out onto the lawn and they played with a big red ball. Fiona loved it, laughed whenever Alice missed a catch. Alice wondered how often Fiona managed to play with other children and decided to take it up with Ben. Was there a nursery school in Soalay—or even just a playgroup? If there wasn't a playgroup, could it be considered part of her job to organise one? She'd have to think about that.

Fiona had her evening meal and then, to give Mrs McCann a rest, Alice bathed her and then read her the bedtime story. A quick kiss on the forehead and soon Fiona was asleep. Alice checked the baby alarm and then went downstairs to wait for Ben.

She was definitely liking her new life, she decided.

She liked being with Fiona. She was staying in a beautiful house, she would shortly have an excellent meal with Ben. And then they would spend a pleasant, uncomplicated evening together. Yes, she was looking forward to being with Ben for a couple of hours. It was as if… She had to stop herself. She was living too much with the memories of the past. Now was now; things were different and she should have learned her lesson. What was thought of as permanent too often was not. You may think you were in love but there was no certainty to it. It was a bitter lesson but she had learned it well. This situation was great—but it could only last a few days.

So when he came home and they sat down for another of Mrs McCann's lovely meals, she decided to try to be a little more formal. He asked her about her day and she said she had a case to discuss with him.

'I went to see a woman called Debbie Laws, who's about thirty-two weeks pregnant. I think I'm going to have problems. She's a primigravida and her husband is insisting that she has the baby at home. Also there's a bit of a history of asthma.'

'A home birth is not a good idea when you're at least an hour from the midwife and there's the risk of asthma. And I've heard of her husband—it's Freddie, isn't it? A man who likes his own opinions.'

'True. If Debbie can't get to the clinic, I shall be visiting her at least every fortnight from now on, and I'll try to convince her. But there's something else. There's a boy there, Albert, a child of Freddie's previous marriage. Aged about seven. Debbie says he's getting more and more tired, sleeps a lot of the time, has been doing so for some weeks. And I just wondered if there might be something a bit serious there. I know children of that age tend to be moody but…'

Ben was obviously interested. 'Anything specific you had in mind?'

'He had difficulty in finding my hand when I held it out to him. Very poor depth perception.'

Now Ben was obviously concerned. 'So you think… a brain problem?'

'I don't think a scan would be a bad idea,' Alice said. 'Of course, I could be completely wrong. I hope I am.' She knew the dangers of making a fast diagnosis when you didn't have all of the facts.

Ben pondered. 'Like I said, I've heard of Freddie Laws. He's got some peculiar ideas. He thinks he's getting near to nature, living up here. Well, he'll have to learn that nature can be harsh and cruel. He thinks that because of the internet, people will just stop working in London and will settle where they like, live how they like. Well, some will, but…'

He reached for his diary, leafed through it. 'It looks like being a bright day tomorrow—how do you fancy a trip out into the countryside as soon as we've finished work? We could drop in and see Albert—nothing official, just in the neighbourhood…'

'I've got some new pamphlets I need to send to Debbie. It'll be an excuse to deliver them in person.'

'Good. If I think Albert needs attention, we lean on Freddie. Two can lean harder than one. But gently, of course. So that Freddie thinks that whatever we decide is his idea.'

Alice laughed. 'Do you know how much you've changed? You used to be a bright lad who thought that if the islanders didn't fall into line, they should be just told what to do. Told by you, the medical expert.'

He laughed himself. 'I've grown older and I've learned. I'm happy in my work and I like the people I work with. After all, I'm one of them. As you are. There's a bond between us. We're both islanders.'

'A bond between us.' She repeated his words because she rather liked them. 'So you don't regret moving back here?'

'Never. I could have earned a lot of money in Edinburgh, but I'd have had no time to spend it and no pleasure in spending it. And I always intended to come back here, you know that. And now you're here, too. Why did you come back?'

Perhaps she was a little more tired than she realised. After all, today had been her first day of real work. So when he casually asked her why she had come back to Soalay, she decided to tell him. Tell him the full story.

'I had loved the work for fifteen years but I suddenly felt that I had to get away from a prestigious London hospital and the staff's cut-throat attitude to promotion. And, of course, I was eased out of my job.'

He had always been a good listener. He leaned over to refill her glass and said, 'Eased out of your job? That seems a bit of a pity. Seems unlikely, too. What happened?'

For some reason, now she'd decided to tell Ben her story, she felt quite comfortable about it. He was a good listener. So… 'I was a high-flyer too. I was running my own department, about to be made Nursing Head of a new centre for both midwifery and child care. Two departments were about to be amalgamated.'

She needed to steady herself a little and took a gulp of her wine. 'Anyway, I had a fiancé, Dr Sean Evans, a paediatric registrar. He worked in my hospital, in my department. I said fiancé but he never really asked me to marry him. We lived together. I just thought we'd get round to it in time. I thought I loved him, and because of that I suppose I overlooked what now seem to be his obvious faults.'

'He was the father of the child you didn't have? Your miscarriage?'

'He was. He seemed to take the miscarriage well, didn't show many signs of grief. At the time I thought he was being strong for both of us. Later I decided…he was relieved.'

Alice made herself lie back in her chair and relax, staring unseeingly at the ceiling. Ben caught her mood, realised she didn't want him to speak.

'Sean was very good-looking, apparently good at his job and I was besotted with him. And both of us were very busy. Perhaps that was why I never really discovered what he was like. Anyway…I was working on a children's ward, he was there with me. A child had an epileptic fit. There was a new drug that had just come onstream. Sean said we'd try it, sent me for it then held the child and told me to inject fifty mil of it. And I did. As I said, we were very busy so I did as I was told, which meant I didn't follow protocol and enter the dose in the child's notes. Sean said he'd do it.'

This was the hard bit. Alice realised she had leaned

forward in her chair, was gripping the arms so tightly that her fingers were white. But she saw Ben's face, his expression calm and yet sympathetic—and it gave her strength. She leaned back again.

'The child calmed at once and Sean left the ward. Five minutes later the child was having much worse convulsions—so bad that I didn't call Sean, I sent for the consultant. He was horrified.'

Somehow she had to calm herself. But the tears ran unchecked down her face. 'The child was brain-damaged and the parents sued the hospital. It was the drug that was the problem—I should have injected ten mil, not fifty. Sean swore that he had told me ten mil. And when we looked at the notes that he had filled in, it did say ten mil. He had filled in the notes while I was still on the ward! Protecting himself!

'And, Ben, sometimes at night I dream of that poor little child. I remember the convulsions and I wake up feeling guilty. I should have checked the dose! It was my job, not Sean's.'

'No, it wasn't your job and you know that! Alice, you did nothing wrong!'

Now, as always, she was angry. 'He appeared sympathetic. But he told everyone that he knew I was over-tired, said he knew I had been suffering because of the miscarriage, he had been worried about my behaviour for a while. I had just made a mistake and part of the blame was his because he should have acted on this. I said I hadn't made a mistake. But who do you believe— a concerned senior doctor or an overtired nurse? I was known to be good but he was senior. Nurses can make mistakes, registrars do not. There was an inquiry and I was found to have been at fault. I was told quietly not to make too much of a fuss, it could only do my career harm. I was reprimanded, he was let off. I had trusted him, both as a medical colleague and as my lover. So much for trust! I felt betrayed, both by the hospital system and by Sean. And one poor little mite was brain-damaged. Can you imagine what it feels like to be blamed for that?'

And then, as it always did, the anger passed. All that was left was deep sadness. 'The parents were very good. They sued but they weren't angry at me. And they said that Sean had been a great comfort to them. Sean, a comfort! That did hurt.'

Her story was more or less over and she fell silent. After a while, Ben asked, 'So you came to Scotland looking for a sanctuary?'

'Yes. Just for a year. I did have one friend, a consultant who believed in me. He told me that there was nothing that could be done now, to go away for a year and there would be a job waiting for me when I came back. I'm looking forward to that.'

'Soalay will heal you,' Ben said. 'When I saw you first, on the ferry, you looked…wounded. And wary. As if you could trust nobody.'

'I was wary and I still am. I needed a haven, some-where where I could work in peace—and where I wouldn't be bothered by men. I don't trust love any more.'

'I know that feeling. But do you think it's possible you've found your haven in Soalay?'

'It's not impossible,' she said after a few minutes' thought. 'I've been very happy since I got here.'

The thought flicked across her consciousness and it almost surprised her. She had been very happy since she'd got to Soalay—and it was due in large part to her spending so much time with Ben. She enjoyed his company so much. And—the realisation took her breath away—it wasn't the memories of fifteen years before. She enjoyed the company of the new Ben, the mature man. A man any girl would be happy to fall in love with.

They were in luck when they arrived at the Lawses' cottage. Freddie had gone for a walk—apparently he had some accounting problems and hoped that the sea air might help him find a solution. Alice gave Debbie the pamphlets she had promised her and then said, 'This is Dr Cavendish. Since we were in the area together, I thought it might be a good idea if the doctor took a quick look at Albert. He seemed a bit peaky when I saw him last.'

She saw Ben wince at the word 'peaky'—but she knew that Debbie would react to it.

Debbie looked doubtful. 'Didn't we ought to wait for Freddie to come back? He is the boy's father and he—'

'I agree, it would be nice if Freddie was here,' Ben said smoothly. 'But I'm afraid we haven't much time. Of course, you are Albert's mother now and as such fully entitled to give your permission to have him examined. You won't want to wait for Freddie's permission when your new baby comes along and you want him examined? Will you?'

'It would be awful if it turned out later that something

was wrong with Albert and you hadn't done anything about it,' Alice put in.

Debbie sighed, realising that she was being manipulated, but she didn't really seem to mind. 'If you'll explain all that to Freddie when he gets back,' she said. 'Come on up. Albert is lying on his bed.'

Debbie sat there as Alice helped Ben with his first examination—the usual BP, pulse, heart rate and so on. And as they examined him they talked to Albert. It was important that they get some idea of how he felt, what interested him. Albert felt tired. He wasn't interested in anything very much.

Alice noticed that Ben paid particular attention to Albert's eyes. He also handed him things from time to time—and asked Albert to stretch out and pick up one of the models sitting on his bedside cabinet. Albert often missed.

'What's happening here? I didn't give you permission to examine my son!'

No one had heard Freddie return from his walk. Now here he was in the doorway of Albert's bedroom. And he was enraged!

'If he's ill, perhaps he needs to see the doctor. It can't really hurt him,' Debbie tried, but Freddie wasn't going to pay too much attention to his wife.

'Doctor whatever your name is! Please leave my son alone and come downstairs and explain yourself.'

'Of course,' said Ben. 'And my name is Dr Cavendish.'

He smiled down at Albert, said, 'That wasn't too bad, was it? Now Nurse Muir here will give you a badge you can pin on your T-shirt and I'll go downstairs and chat to your father. You get some more rest.' Alice noticed that Ben carefully closed the bedroom door after they had all left.

The four adults trooped downstairs. 'I thought that yesterday I made it quite clear to the midwife here that there is nothing wrong with Albert. She is in our home as a midwife, that is all. I am not interested in her opinions on the health of my son.' Obviously Freddie was not going to be placated easily.

'Miss Muir is an experienced registered children's nurse as well as a midwife,' Ben said, 'and you may shortly have to thank her for her skills. She spotted something that needs to be investigated. That child should have received medical attention long before today.'

Alice hid a smile as she remembered the decision made the night before. If necessary, they would lean on Freddie—but lean gently so that he thought that whatever was decided was his idea. If this was Ben's idea of gentle…

But… 'And what does the experienced children's nurse think is wrong with Albert?' Freddie was being sarcastic.

'The experienced children's nurse thinks the same as I do. First, we desperately hope that nothing is seriously wrong. And that could be true. But, secondly, we think that there is the possibility of some malfunction of the brain. And that needs to be investigated.'

'Rubbish,' said Freddie. Alice thought that there wasn't the same certainty as there had been. But then Freddie thought of another tack. 'Anyway, if Albert is to be seen by a doctor, I'd prefer to have him seen privately.'

'That is, of course, your right. But I shall expect a letter from an accredited medical professional in the next three or four days, stating that Albert is receiving attention, otherwise I shall have no alternative but to inform the police that I believe Albert is being abused.'

'Abused! What are you talking about?' Freddie's disbelief, his horror were all too obvious.

'Any child who is denied necessary medical attention is being abused. Mr Laws, please don't think I'm joking. We take child abuse very seriously up here.'

Alice had never seen a man deflate so quickly. There was silence in the room for a while, and then Freddie said, in a much quieter voice, 'What do you think is necessary?'

'Albert needs to be seen by a consultant paediatric neurologist. He'll have to be tested—CT and MRI scans will be only the beginning. As I said, there may be nothing amiss. But if there is, action is needed at once.'

'What's the next step?'

'I think that speed is of the essence now. If you want me to handle it, I'll phone the mainland hospital tomorrow. Albert could be being examined a couple of days after that. Someone will have to go with him, of course.'

'Right. So…can you phone?'

'As I said, I'll do so tomorrow.'

Alice felt not happy but satisfied as they drove back towards Soalay and she thought that Ben felt the same way too. They had done right by Albert. They had acted as medical professionals. She only hoped that, if there was anything wrong, it wasn't too late to put it right.

So she looked out of the window and smiled her

pleasure. The Soalay landscape was part of her birth-right. She had come back to reclaim it. 'Look,' she said, 'there's Ben Sleatan. Remember we climbed to the top of it? It was so hot when we got to the top and you...' Then her voice trailed away. She was remembering.

She glanced sideways. Ben's face was set. 'I think I remember,' he said. 'Remember vaguely. But that was a long time ago.'

She knew he wasn't telling the truth. He did re-member. What had happened had been so wonderful, so important to them. And now he was frightened of what the memories might bring back.

It had been hot. They had climbed the mountain and they had been entirely alone—no one to be seen for miles. At the summit they had rested on a tiny patch of grass, he had taken off his T-shirt. 'Now that feels better,' he had said. Then he had looked at her, smiling but with a challenging look in his eye. So, daringly, she had taken off her own T-shirt. It had felt strangely lib-erating. And when he had kissed her, he had undone her simple cotton bra. Well, he had tried to. Not the easiest thing to do with one hand. So eventually she had helped him. She had felt so bold and so happy!

They had lain side by side, kissing. She had never felt anything so exciting as the touch of his skin on her bare breasts. But then he had moved a little and kissed her there...

Alice put the memory from her and sighed. She could guess what was going through his mind now. He was frightened of getting too close to her, of bringing out the kind of feelings that had caused him so much pain. The kind of feelings that he'd had for his wife. And she couldn't blame him. In her turn she was frightened of getting close to him.

She liked his company, which made it hard living with him. She was still fearful of what her feelings could cost her. And what about her vows of treating this place as a man-free sanctuary for a year, of having nothing to do with men? Perhaps, too, she was getting too fond of Fiona. Ben and Fiona were a definite package.

She decided not to think further about things, let Ben make any decisions about their relationship. But Ben didn't seem to want to move on from the state they were in now.

And did she? Well, she could be tempted.

CHAPTER SIX

So this was it and she liked it. Home. Well, home at least for a year. When she had parted from Sean she had promptly moved out of the flat they had shared and into a rented room offered by the hospital. It had been pleasant enough but not really somewhere to call home. For too long she had needed a place where she felt she belonged. She needed a home and this was nearly it.

She had just moved into the flat above her clinic. Her three trunks had been delivered, she had been living out of a suitcase for too long. Her clothes were now in the built-in wardrobe, her books were on the shelves, there were pictures on the wall. She had even paid a visit to the new supermarket and stocked up her larder.

She was hot and pleasantly weary. It was early evening now and she decided that what she needed was a bath and a cup of tea. But first she wandered around her new domain, thinking how much larger it looked now that there was no builders' clutter.

It was only a small flat but the light-painted walls and the large windows made it seem larger. And she had to admit that the furnishings were minimal but very comfortable. Someone's taste was very similar to her own. Ben's taste—he had chosen the furniture. Another indication that they had so much in common…

Yes, she knew she was going to be happy here.

'Sorry things have taken longer than I thought,' Henry the builder had said, 'but I wanted to get things just right, try to get rid of the smell of paint.' He had pressed a card into her hand. 'Any problem, night or day, give me a call.'

'Thanks Henry, I will.'

He had done a good job. Secretly, she had wondered if Ben had talked him into slowing down a little. It had been a fortnight and there hadn't seemed to be too much work to do. But what did she know about building? And why would Ben want her to stay longer at his home?

She had really enjoyed staying with him and felt that he had enjoyed her company too. But after that first welcoming kiss on the quayside there had been no further advances. Of course, he was an honourable man, he might have felt that it was wrong even to try to kiss her when she was a guest in his house. It would have been taking advantage of her. But she felt he might at least have given her a goodnight kiss. She had to admit being envious when he took Fiona in his arms and hugged her. And she thought that once or twice she had caught him looking at her as if he wanted to… Foolish thoughts!

She had to admit to herself that although she was so happy to be moving here into her own place, she still very much regretted having to leave Taighean dhe Gaoithe. 'You will come and see us?' Mrs McCann had asked anxiously. 'Wee Fiona will miss you.'

'I'll miss her and I'll miss your cooking, Mrs

McCann. But I really need to be living nearer the job. And what would people say if they knew that my flat was finished and that I was still staying with Dr Cavendish?'

'True,' Mrs McCann said judiciously. 'But…'

She never finished the sentence so Alice didn't know what the 'but' meant.

She was here and she was happy.

The bath was nearly full and Alice was just deciding which of the lined-up bath oils to squirt in. Her doorbell rang and when she went down to answer it there was a delivery man with a large bouquet of flowers. Delighted, she took them inside. It had been years since someone had given her flowers.

There was a note inside. 'Welcome to your new home. We hope you'll be happy in it. Love from Ben, Fiona and Mrs McCann.' The flowers were lilies, her favourites. Overwhelmed, Alice took them upstairs, put them straight in water. They looked so good!

Lilies. She was astonished that Ben had remembered that they were her favourite flower—he had bought her a bunch for her seventeenth birthday. For a while she sat just looking at them. Then she made her tea and went to get into her bath.

Her bath. As she sat there surrounded by tendrils of steam, the smell of lavender from the bath oil calming her, she felt at home. Although she had loved living with Ben, she now felt that she had her own roots. She wasn't a guest, not obliged to anyone, she was her own mistress. This flat, even though the furnishings had been ordered by Ben, was not in his gift. It had come to her from the trust. And because of this she felt she could approach Ben more as an equal. She could make her own decision about living. Which meant she could invite him to dinner. Invite Ben to dinner? What a good idea! What a courteous thing to do after she had lived with him for a fortnight! She turned the hot tap on with her big toe.

Later, she sat in her dressing-gown and rather apprehensively phoned him at home. It had only been a few hours since she had last seen him. But when she heard his voice over the telephone, it still thrilled her. 'Ben? Alice here. I'm phoning you to thank you for the flowers. They are truly lovely. And you remembered they are my favourites.'

'I love lilies myself. Can you remember how I cunningly found out they were your favourites? All those years ago?'

She giggled. 'Yes. You didn't know me all that well, we'd only just…just got together. We were at school and I was sketching and you asked me what my favourite colour was. And what colour flower. Then I was a bit miffed because you said you couldn't spend Saturday with me. It turned out that you'd taken the ferry to the mainland and then come straight back 'cos there were no lilies in the shop here. I thought that was wonderful.'

'Things are different here now, more complicated. We've all moved on. There was no difficulty in buying lilies locally and we're not seventeen any more. Everything is more complicated.'

'Isn't it just?' she said. 'Now I'm settled in the flat and I know I'm going to be very happy here. But I'll still miss Fiona and Mrs McCann and you. I had a wonderful stay with you and I'd like to say thank you. Would you like to come to dinner one night?'

'What? All three of us?'

She laughed. 'No, it will have to be well after Fiona's bedtime. I thought just you. A supper to thank you for all of Mrs McCann's dinners. No big thing, we both have to work the next day.'

'And I'd love to come. When?'

She made a snap decision. Why hang about? 'Tomorrow night?' she asked, hoping he couldn't detect the nervousness in her voice.

'I'm looking forward to it.'

She had been working full time for a week now, had organised her clinics, her home visits, had delivered her first baby in the new birthing unit. There was plenty of work—and she guessed there soon would be more. It was all enjoyable.

Sometimes she would see a lot of Ben during the day, sometimes she would hardly see him at all. Twice she had called him over for a second opinion—each time he had agreed with her diagnosis. Today she hadn't seen him once. A busy day for both of them.

He was coming at eight. She had spent most of her spare time since she'd phoned him on planning and replanning the menu. And there had to be another visit to the supermarket. But she was ready when he came.

She had decided that this was going to be more than just a little supper—this was going to be an almost formal event. She had managed to finish the cooking and lay the table an hour before he was due to arrive. There was time to have a quick shower, shampoo her hair, put on a dress that had only just arrived—sleeveless, in dark blue silk. It wasn't exactly an evening dress but it looked a bit special. She took extra care with her hair and make-up and reminded herself to ask around for the best hairdresser.

Then she sat and waited. It was necessary to be calm when he arrived. She wondered why her heart was beating so quickly and told herself that it was because she had not prepared for this kind of an occasion for quite a while. But he was just an old friend, nothing more. He had helped her, she was saying thank you. That was all.

But when she heard the car draw up outside her heart started beating quickly again.

She opened the door, smiled. She could see that he too had made an effort to dress suitably. And he had got it just right, half casual, half formal. He was wearing dark trousers and a white silk shirt. The white silk set off his slightly weatherbeaten skin. He looked gorgeous. For a moment they looked at each other, Alice wondered if he was feeling the same as she was.

He handed her a bottle. 'Not more flowers but champagne,' he said. 'For a beautiful lady.'

'Champagne! What are we celebrating?'

'The island's good luck in having a new midwife and children's nurse. And my good luck as having you as a…partner?'

'Right,' she said, blushing slightly. 'Well, do come in.'

He looked round approvingly as they entered her

living room. 'What a difference! You've made this a real home. It's you.'

'It's just as much you,' she told him. 'I gather you had a large hand in picking the paint and the furnishings.'

He shrugged. 'I did what I could.'

She had to agree that the room did look particularly attractive. She had put candles on the little table but the evening sun was still shining through the window, making the cutlery and the glassware glint.

'I bought some wine but since you've brought it, shall we start on the champagne?' she asked. 'Will you open it?' She felt a little uneasy. This was now her home, he was her guest. Would things be different between them?

Expertly, he opened the champagne, filled two glasses. He handed one to her. She accepted it and then waved a hand, indicating that he sit on the couch. Then she sat in her easy chair, opposite him not next to him.

Perhaps he felt her unease. He started to talk, easily, interestingly, about his day's work, about the island and how it had changed in the past fifteen years. So Alice quickly relaxed. He was an old friend, they were talking as old friends did who were interested in each other. She also felt better after she had finished her glass of champagne. It went to her head. She realised that in the rush to prepare for this evening she hadn't eaten since breakfast. Whatever the reason, after fifteen minutes she felt more confident.

Later, she wondered if she had been over-confident. Perhaps the champagne had affected her more than she'd known. But they were old friends and so she said, 'Ben, you know most of my secret life and now I want to know yours. You know things about me that no other people here know. And I feel a bit vulnerable. So I want to know about you. Please, will you tell me about your divorce?' Then she realised what she had said, gulped and muttered, 'Sorry, I'm a bit overtired and I must have—'

He laughed. 'Like you said, we're old friends. And there's no one I'd more happily tell than you.' But she noticed that he filled their glasses again before he started to talk. She thought this was going to be an ordeal for him.

'You don't have to tell me,' she said. 'I want this evening to be something that you really enjoy.'

His voice was gentle. 'Alice, I intend to enjoy it.'

But it still took him some time to start. 'Fiona's birth was…well, it would be wrong to say it was an accident, 'cos the result has been so marvellous. But it wasn't exactly planned—at least, not by me. Melissa, Fiona's mother, tricked me. The oldest trick in the world. She said she was on the Pill—but she wasn't. And I didn't know that she was pregnant until it was far too late.'

He was quiet a moment. 'You don't seem too angry about it now,' Alice ventured. 'You seem quite calm.'

'I've made myself be calm. I've learned my lesson, even though it was a hard one.'

He sipped his drink and went on, 'She was quite a senior nurse. We had met in Edinburgh when I was a medical student and then we met again when I was back in the city on a medical refresher course a few years ago. We got on together and…' He shrugged. 'I found she was pregnant and eventually we got married. I brought her back to Soalay and she hated it. I had told her what life was like here, even brought her to look around. But once we got here she just wasn't having it.'

'Why didn't she realise what it was like when she came the first time?'

'I suspect that she thought that I wouldn't marry her if she refused to live here with me. The trouble was, she knew I'd been offered a partnership in a practice in Edinburgh. A firm I'd worked with before, I'd been a GP registrar there. Plenty of private work. I could have doubled, even trebled my NHS salary. We'd be rich, she said. She wouldn't have to work again. And she told me she hated this house.'

When she'd first known him Ben had been a calm, controlled person. He hadn't lost his temper easily, he'd managed to convey what he'd felt forcefully but somehow quietly. But Alice had always known what he'd been feeling. There would be a glint in his eyes, his speech became more clipped. She knew that the story he was telling now had hurt him.

'What about when Fiona was born?' she asked. 'I've seen it before, you must have too. A woman might not be too keen on having a baby, but when it finally comes everything changes.'

'Not Melissa.' Alice was shocked at the bitterness in his tone. 'Melissa tried to use the baby to blackmail me, make me move back to Edinburgh. She said she'd go herself and take Fiona with her… The hardest thing I ever did in my life was call her bluff. I said I wouldn't move.'

He shook his head. For a moment he was again the eighteen-year-old boy Alice had known, and her heart went out to him in a wave of sympathy that was astonishing in its strength.

'So what happened?'

'It was nothing I did, I was just lucky. Melissa had gone to Edinburgh—she said to see old friends. Leaving Fiona behind, of course. The so-called old friends persuaded her to stay. I was happy with her away. I had Fiona. And after a while I had a letter saying that she had met a man, a South African surgeon who would really look after her. The kind of man she had thought I was going to be.'

'What kind of man was that?'

'A rich man,' Ben said with a sardonic smile. 'But he was the kind of man that suited me. He wanted Melissa—but not a baby. So I got to keep Fiona but lose Melissa. It was better than winning the lottery. I had the best advocates in Edinburgh to organize the divorce, ensure that Fiona was legally and entirely mine. Her mother now has no claim on her at all. And I am happy. In fact, everyone's happy, even Melissa.'

There was just one question Alice had to ask. 'Has all this…altered you at all?' she asked.

'It's taught me that I don't need a wife to be happy. Fiona is all I need.'

'I see,' Alice said. She thought she saw all too well. She managed to mutter, 'I'll just go and see how things are doing in the kitchen.'

As she well knew, everything was fine in the kitchen. But she pottered about in there for five minutes. She needed to calm down. She had been looking forward so much to this evening, it had to be a success. Which meant she had to be in the right mood. What Ben had just said had upset her. Had upset her a lot! But she was going to get over it!

When she was ready she called out, 'Would you like to eat now?'

'I would indeed.'

'It'll be different from Mrs McCann's cooking.'

'I love Mrs McCann's cooking but an occasional change would be no bad thing.'

Alice giggled. 'I have to confess, I put on two pounds while staying with you.'

'You look better for it,' he said. 'Alice, that's not meant as a compliment, it's an observation. I think you look less…less distracted than you did when you got off the ferry.'

'That's certainly due to Mrs McCann's cooking. Now, you must try my cooking.' She did not want to talk about how she had looked when she first came to the island.

The first course was OK, unexceptionable. Grilled, herbed chicken breast with a simple salad of tomatoes and rocket. They talked happily as they ate, she knew it was all right. But the next course was something else.

She fetched in two warmed plates and then placed a large earthenware pot in the centre of the table. In a strained voice she said, 'This is my signature dish. I've made it often—but I try to make it a bit different each time. It's simple but it's…well, it means a lot to me. Help yourself while I fetch the garlic bread.'

She lifted the lid and passed him a serving spoon. But she didn't go into the kitchen.

He leaned forward, smelled. Alice had to admit it

smelled good. It was basically a peasant dish. There was fried rice, a variety of chopped vegetables and two cut-up sirloin steaks. But the secret was in the herbs and spices.

He looked at her, she looked back, there was a moment of communion between them. Both of them remembered. 'You cooked this dish for me before,' he said. 'It was the night of the school dance. Your parents were away on the mainland so you invited me over. You got the recipe out of a book because you'd never cooked anything like this before. And I had bought a bottle of wine. Not a very expensive one, I'm afraid but it was all the shop had.'

'To me it was lovely. It might have cost just a tenth the price of this bottle of champagne—but to me it tasted just as good.'

'To me as well.'

Alice wondered if smells were more efficient in calling back memories than anything else. As so often before since she had returned to the island, memories came flooding back. 'We drank it all. Then we… I took you to my bedroom and for the first time we…'

'We went to sleep afterwards,' he said softly. 'Then I had to wake up in a panic to go home. My parents knew I'd be late—but if I didn't get home at all I thought they would worry.'

Another moment of shared reflections. Then she rose and said, 'Well, I didn't cook it to let it go cold. I'll fetch the bread while you help yourself.'

'And I'll fill your glass.' He reached for the champagne bottle. 'I'm really looking forward to this.'

In the kitchen she bent to slide the warming bread out

of the oven. She knew he'd enjoy the dish she had prepared. Everyone did. Everyone except Sean, that was. He didn't like it because it didn't have potatoes. He thought rice belonged only in puddings. He had attended a good boarding school.

She sat opposite Ben and ate, and mysteriously she was seventeen again, having cooked for the man in her life. The man now sitting with her. She didn't ask what he was thinking, feeling—she thought she knew. And he said little, too.

To follow there was a simple fruit salad and she had bought some tremendously expensive coffee for after that. But in the middle of eating the salad, his mobile rang.

'I should have switched it off,' he said. He took out the phone, looked at it gloomily, let it ring.

'You've got to answer it, you're a doctor. In fact, you're *the* doctor.'

'I know I am and I know I've got to answer.' he looked at the screen and sighed. 'And this is important—it's Sergeant Cullen.'

'Hi, Sergeant, Dr Cavendish here… How long ago? How many? Do you think we need to send for a helicopter? OK, I'm in town and I'm on my way.'

He clicked his phone shut. 'Accident in the docks,' he said. 'Two men caught between the dockside and their ship, bodies partly crushed. I've got to go. It sounds like a long job.'

'Do you want me to come with you?'

'No. I might call out Morag but you'll be needed to hold the fort here tomorrow.'

'Do you want to go next door and pick up a medical kit?'

But even as she asked, she knew the answer. 'No. There's one in the car, I never drive anywhere without it. Alice, this is the worst ending to the evening. I was enjoying myself so much and things were going so well between us.'

'Off you go,' she said. 'Shall I phone Mrs McCann to say you're going to be late?'

'Thanks, that would be a good idea.'

She could tell how torn he was—which meant that he felt the same as she did. 'Don't worry. You can come again some time—some time soon. Now, let's get you off.'

She accompanied him down to the front door, thinking that their evening was over. Certainly she wasn't expecting what happened next.

He kissed her. Not a friendly kiss or the dutiful kiss from a guest to a host but a real kiss. For a moment she was wrapped up in the wonder of it and when he let her go she stared up at him as if dazed. Feelings only vaguely remembered came crashing back. He used to kiss her like that and she…

Slowly, sadly, he took his lips from hers but still held her. 'It may not be much,' he said hoarsely. 'Perhaps I can come back and have coffee.'

She pushed him away gently. 'Don't hope, don't even think about it,' she said. 'If it's possible then I'd love you to…but you're a doctor, you know what's going to happen.'

For a moment she thought he was going to add something. But instead he just nodded. 'True.' Then he turned and was gone. Alice watched his car drive away and sighed.

She went back to her living room, looked at the remnants of their meal. They looked sad, deserted. This wasn't the way this evening was meant to end, she thought. But end this way it had. Still…it hadn't been a complete disaster. Or had it? It had restarted ideas, thoughts that had been only idly buzzing around in her head. And how had she wanted, expected the evening to end? She realised that she hadn't even thought about that. She had thought about the beginning…but the rest she had never even contemplated.

What to do now? Well, she had cooked this meal— there was no way she was going not to enjoy it to its full. He wasn't with her, she would imagine that he was. So she sat, ate the rest of her fruit salad. Then she went to percolate her expensive coffee, and while it was bubbling through the machine she picked out a CD and put it in her player. Another joke. It was a CD that they had enjoyed together all those years before.

She drank her coffee, it was good. The CD came to an end and she sighed. She already did know but…there was no way he was going to come back now.

She changed out of her blue party dress and started to clear away. As she did so her phone rang. Her heart started to pound. There were few people who knew her number, not many people would phone her, he might be… It was Sergeant Cullen. 'Dr Cavendish asked me to phone you. Apparently we dragged him away while the two of you were checking some of your new equipment.'

Well, you could call it that, Alice thought. But she said, 'No problem, Sergeant. We can do it again another time.'

'Good. Well, his message is that we're taking one of the injured men over to the mainland by boat. We don't want the expense of a helicopter. The doctor wants to stay with the man. He'll be back early tomorrow morning.'

'I'll see that his family is told. Thank you, Sergeant.' She replaced the receiver and sighed. Well, it had been a vain hope.

Mechanically she put some dishes away, pushed others into the dishwasher. Simple domestic jobs stopped her thinking, she needed the discipline. But eventually her flat was as spotless as it had been when she'd first entered it and it was still not time for bed.

She had a shower, put on her nightgown. Another CD and a book? Then she remembered the champagne in the fridge. She'd have a last glass. There was no way she would go to sleep now. Not after the unfinished way the evening had ended. But there had been the kiss! It had been the kiss of a lover, she was sure. Certainly she had responded as a lover. Or had it just been the kiss of a man who had been angry at being interrupted in the middle of a pleasant evening? She didn't know. Had the kiss been meant to tell her something or had it just been a kiss? She didn't know.

So she sat, sipped her champagne and remembered the first time she had cooked that very same dish for Ben.

It had been after the school summer dance. Alice had felt beautiful, she'd had that inner glow that came from knowing she'd been wanted, the sole object of Ben's desire. The evening had retained the summer heat, so she had worn a simple strapless summer dress. The gossamer, sea-coloured fabric had shown off her skin and revealed the tops of her breasts, tanned a light gold. Her mother had grown out of the dress and had been glad to see how lovely Alice had looked in it. She'd said, 'You look like a sea nymph, all energy and big eyes.'

The dress had been perfect for the summer dance. He'd held her close all night, stroking the bare skin of her shoulders, lightly kissing her forehead and resting his head against hers. She had been so happy, filled with the renewed knowledge of her power over him. At the last dance, they'd clung tightly to each other, Alice breathing in the warm smell of his body, revelling in being held in his arms. She'd nestled under his chin, sensing the echo of his voice as her head had rested against his chest. She had been living just for the sensations of the moment, no thought about future or past, no worries or cares.

That had been then. She smiled to remember the carefree girl she had been. Ben too had been an innocent, a boy, sincere and honest and full of desire for her. Not like Sean…

They set off back to Alice's house. Earlier she'd prepared a supper for him and left it ready, knowing they'd be starving after the dance. Her parents were away, and Alice wanted Ben to admire the first proper meal she'd cooked for him. Then she meant to send him home, after they'd kissed and perhaps explored each other a little. Just playing as usual, nothing really serious. She knew they would stop before doing anything she might regret.

She'd shied away from thinking about what Ben might really want to do, what part of her wanted him to do. But she was a good island girl. She knew too much would change too soon if they slept together now.

Now the adult Alice realised that the heightened emotions they'd felt that night had meant that what had followed had been inevitable.

The supper had been wonderful—just a casserole, one dish in case they were hungry when they came back from the dance. The idea had been to cook something simple, something she could pass off as being a dish she had hastily thrown together while preparing for the dance. In fact, she had spent hours scouring cookery books for a suitable recipe. Then there had been buying, or sending off for, the ingredients. She had spent as much time preparing this so-called simple dish as she had making herself ready for the dance. But it had been worth it. And they had drunk the bottle of wine he had brought.

Afterwards she sat by him on the couch, and he stroked the slopes of her breasts, the swell of her stomach. She wanted the ache, the fevered warmth that infused her skin to continue, wanted the urgent kisses he was showering on her. He was clumsy with need, almost hurting with his passion. She kissed him back, harder and more urgently than she'd thought she was capable of. She didn't mind the roughness of his chin, loved the feeling of being carried away on a tide of feelings, the feel of unfamiliar skin-to-skin contact. She knew that she could stop him, knew that she might regret her decision, knew that she wanted him more than she'd ever wanted anything in her life.

'Ben, Ben, I want you,' she said softly, somehow knowing that he needed her to say it was all right, needed her permission. She wriggled down the couch and pulled him towards her. His body was rigid, trembling with the tension and excitement of this moment.

'Alice,' he said, 'Alice, show me your bedroom.'

'Why?' She knew it was a stupid question.

'I want to be able to imagine you in it when I'm alone and lonely in mine,' he said. 'But most of all I want to lie with you and tell you how you make me feel…'

So she showed him her bedroom.

He had obviously thought about this, he had precautions ready, she wouldn't get pregnant. Knowing this made her love him more than ever. But then the first time was over so quickly. Afterwards Ben seemed a little guilty or ashamed, but mainly full of pride, satisfaction and most of all tender gratitude and wonderment at Alice.

She had wondered how she'd feel. Other girls had said that the first time usually wasn't so good, but she had felt full of love, and had taken her pleasure in his pleasure. It didn't seem to matter that she still felt that warm ache. She was happy, happy in the moment, wanted nothing except for this night to continue for ever.

She wanted to tell him that it had been amazing, that how she felt had been so special, that he had been everything she could have wanted of him, but she couldn't find the words, was oddly shy with him.

He seemed to sense her doubts. 'Alice, are you all right? What we've just done, it was so… I mean, are you…?'

'Ben, it was what I wanted and you've made me so happy. Now lie here with me for a while longer.'

So they lay together. But after a while he reached for her with new confidence and what they did together then made the ache in her body grow and then explode in a cascade of feelings that she had never thought possible.

There was one last thing she remembered—perhaps the most important thing. They were lying side by side, holding hands. Still in awe of what they had just discovered. But there was something she had to say to him. She had—they both had—the teenage fear of putting anything into words.

'Alice, that was so wonderful,' he mumbled. 'I was hoping but I didn't think it would be anything like this, and now I know that I…'

She leaned over, put a finger over his lips. 'We're both young, Ben. We'll have careers to follow soon, we're not to make any stupid commitments that we could regret later.'

He took her finger in his hands, kissed it. 'I was going to say that I loved you and that I wanted to—'

'No! You're not to say anything! What we have just had is to remain on its own and perfect. We're to keep it and treasure it but we aren't to talk about it. Now you can kiss me again if you want.'

So he hadn't said any more. And whatever her feelings were for him, she had kept them quiet too. That had been so many years ago. And now she wished she had said something then—or allowed him to say something. Allowed him to say that he loved her. Of course, now, fifteen years later, he still could say that he loved her. If he wanted to.

Her eyelids were closing, too much emotion was

tiring. She sipped the last of the champagne, cleaned her teeth and went to bed. But as she slipped into sleep one last thought crossed her mind. She had loved Ben fifteen years ago, though she had never said so. And now she was learning to love him again. She was asleep before she could take the thought further.

CHAPTER SEVEN

THE thought was with her when she woke up next morning. She looked at the sunlight penetrating her curtains, heard the screaming of gulls. Common early morning experiences in summer. But why did they please her so much? Why did she feel so happy?

In fact, she felt the happiness before she worked out why. It had been her last thought the night before. That last minute realisation of something that should have been obvious much earlier. She was falling in love with Ben. Or falling in love with Ben again. Re-falling in love?

So what was she to do about it? Love wasn't the reason she had come to Soalay, she had needed a refuge where she could find peace. Love didn't bring peace. Especially if it wasn't—as far as she could tell—returned.

She sighed as she climbed out of bed. At the moment there was nothing she could do. She would just have to wait and see. And work, of course.

That morning she held a clinic. Four pregnant women from town came in for routine checks. They were all in the last ten weeks of pregnancy and at that stage Alice liked to see her patients at least once a fortnight. And she told them that if ever there was any cause for alarm to phone her.

They were just routine checks. Blood pressure, pulse, urine sample. More important was to listen to the foetal heart, to palpate the abdomen to ensure that all was going well with the baby. And the constant vigilance to avoid pre-eclampsia—an over-high BP and oedema or swelling, especially of the legs.

What Alice thought was probably most important was the talk she had with the mother-to-be. She would ask about diet, plans for the birth, fears that the mother might have. And it was amazing what important details could come out in the middle of what seemed to be just a casual chat. The trouble was, she sometimes heard things she didn't want to hear.

The first three mums were fine. Two of them remembered her—vaguely. Alice enjoyed talking to them, felt she was doing her job. The fourth, Merryl Snaith, was a bit different. She was an incomer from the mainland, had been left a house by an old relation and decided to move in. She was a single mother and a bit flash for Soalay. The other mothers-to-be were a bit wary of her. She seemed to wear a bit too much lipstick for a visit to the midwife.

'I've been seeing Dr Cavendish up to now,' Merryl told her. 'I decided that if we didn't have a proper midwife then I'd rather see a doctor than a nurse.'

'Nurse Watson has probably dealt with far more pregnant women than Dr Cavendish.'

Alice knew her voice was chill, she couldn't help it.

But Merryl seemed neither to notice or to care. 'Well, please, give the doctor my good wishes.' A quick, alert look and then, 'I heard that you've been staying with the doctor? Isn't it a pity, him separating from his wife?'

Alice knew there was no possibility of keeping secrets on the island, little chance of stopping gossip.

'I'm very fond of his little girl,' she told Merryl. 'I drop in at the house quite frequently to see her. Now, would you like to undress behind that screen and then lie on the couch?'

'Whatever,' said the disappointed Merryl.

But, still, she was happy with her morning's work. She was doing what she liked, what she knew she was good at. And the Merryls of the world only made the other mums more appealing.

After she had finished her first set of examinations, her receptionist gave her a message. Could she phone Dr Cavendish, please? No panic, only when it was convenient. Alice knew when he tried to have his coffee-break so she rang him then. Of course, it would probably be something professional, perhaps someone he wanted to refer to her. Or perhaps he wanted to tell her about the excitement of the night before. Whatever it was, she could feel her heart beating faster and she knew that her cheeks were flushed. She loved talking to him! Still, she had to be professional!

'All go well last night?' she asked him. 'I got your message from Sergeant Cullen.'

'All went more or less well. I got to the harbour just in time, one man had a fractured femur and I had to reduce the fracture. Otherwise he could have lost the leg. But we got him to hospital in time and he should be OK. No one who has been drinking should go anywhere near a fishing boat banging against a harbour wall!'

'Seems to be an obvious truth. But how are you?'

'A bit tired but that's part of a doctor's life, we all know that. Now, I've got a problem. I don't know if it's a personal or a professional problem and whether it's for you or for me. Mostly I think it's an island problem— where everyone knows everyone else. It's not strictly your work, but I could do with a hand.'

'Whatever I can do, I will.' She felt a small thrill. He thought there were things that she could do that he could not.

'Right. Remember a girl called Ann Fairing? She was in your class at school.'

Alice thought back and after a moment did remember. 'Yes. She was a small, quiet girl. She was never a particular friend of mine but we got on well enough. I think we liked each other. People used to call her Mouse because she was so quiet. But I've not seen her or heard of her for fifteen years.'

'Well I've seen quite a bit of her. She's now Mrs McCann, our Mrs McCann's daughter-in-law. She came in earlier today, claiming she wasn't sleeping, the tablets I'd prescribed weren't strong enough. She wanted the tranquillisers that I wouldn't give her, she was worried about her husband, who's a soldier away in the Middle East.'

'And she's worried about her husband getting killed? Well, that's fair enough.'

'I don't think she's worried about him getting killed. Apparently he's got quite a safe job.'

'Perhaps she's just missing him? I could sympathise with that.'

'Me, too. She's got two young children but she seems to be coping with them quite well.' Ben sounded puzzled, she thought. He went on, 'She asked something quite peculiar. She asked if there was any way her prescriptions could be sent in by post. I told her there was no need, there was only one pharmacist on the island but she ought to know that he was very good. But it didn't seem to please her.'

'Odd,' Alice said. 'What do you want me to do?'

'Well, she knew you were back. I told her that I could tell that there was something that she didn't want to discuss with me—perhaps because I was a family friend. But why didn't she drop round and have a word with you? I said it might be something to do with a specifically female problem and in that case you might be able to help. I'd like to know what's wrong and I think you might be able to get it out of her.'

Suddenly, Alice felt in trouble. She could have done without this kind of problem. 'Ben, are you asking me to do something that could be called unprofessional? It sounds like that. This is a terrible thing to say but I told you, I've just been through a hard time because I trusted a man—in fact, I loved him—and he betrayed me.'

There was silence. Then, his voice formal, he said, 'Of course, Alice, it was very wrong of me to ask you. If she does come to see you, tell her it sounds like a problem for the doctor, not you.'

'Ben! Don't be silly! Of course I want to help. And you…you are nothing like Sean Evans. Look, leave it with me and I'll do what I can.'

'That's the Alice Muir I thought I knew.' And he rang off.

Then he rang back again five minutes later. 'Alice, I don't know whether this is good news or bad news—but you need to be proud of yourself.'

'That's nice,' she said, feeling a little jerk of excitement at the compliment.

'I've just heard from the mainland hospital, the people who have been looking at Albert Laws. They've found a meningioma on his sphenoidal ridge. The surgeon thinks he can excise it.'

'A meningioma! That's a benign tumour, isn't it?'

'It's benign. But any tumour in the skull is going to cause problems. The operation will last ten or twelve hours.'

Alice shuddered. This was a branch of medicine she hadn't dealt with for quite a while. 'Well, I'm glad we got to Albert in time. How successful…? I mean…'

'The surgeon is very hopeful and he's known to be a good man. Seventy per cent of these cases died forty years ago, now we're down to thirty per cent. That is good progress.'

'And how is Freddie?'

'It was Freddie who phoned me. Actually, he's quite a devoted father. He doesn't like being wrong—but he asked me to pass on his thanks to you.'

'Well, that's something. I think I'll strike while I have the advantage. I'll phone and tell him that he has to make sure that Debbie comes into the birthing unit, instead of having a home delivery.'

'Great idea. You're a good nurse, Alice Muir,' Ben said, and rang off. Alice felt a throb of delight at the praise.

She thought about Ann Fairing—now Ann McCann— all through her lunch-break. At first she couldn't think of her as Ann, she had to think of her as Mouse. But then she realized this was now a mature woman with two children. Mouse had been a schoolgirl nickname—and not a very complimentary one. Now she must think of her as Ann.

When she sat at her desk again she looked through her notes and found the details of Ann's two children— the injections they'd been given, the inspections they'd had. Not much wrong at all—but she could always make something sound a little worse. She rang Ann.

'I see from his notes that your boy Alec had a bit of a problem with a rash that wouldn't go away. Has it gone now?'

Ann's voice was wary. 'He's had no trouble for a few months. Do you want to see him?'

'I doubt that is necessary. But why don't you call round for a chat? Could you come this afternoon? At any time?'

'I think I'd like that. Yes, I'll come.'

Alice frowned as she rang off. There was something wrong, she could tell from Ann's voice.

Ann was nervous—it was more than that, Ann was worried to death. Her face was pale, she fiddled con- stantly with her handbag. She wouldn't tell Alice why she had come, instead she kept referring back to happier days at school. She wouldn't talk about her husband and when Alice asked about him, she looked even more pale. But Alice felt that she loved him. So what could Alice do to gain her confidence?

Eventually Ann gave her a lead. 'But why are you back here, Alice? I heard on the grapevine that you were doing really well in London. What brought you back to a little place like this?'

Alice decided that if you want to get you had to give. A confidence for a confidence. 'I'll tell you a secret, Ann. I made a big mistake. The usual one—man trouble. I picked the wrong one. Then he got me into trouble at work and I felt I had to leave. And I'd just had a miscarriage so I needed a change. A haven. Somewhere where there was no trouble, and I think this place is it. I can be quiet and happy here.'

'Quiet and happy,' Ann said. 'That seems good.'

Alice saw her flinch. 'Why not tell me, Ann?' she said. 'I know there's something wrong and you know that you've got to tell someone. Tell an old school friend.'

Finally Ann broke down. She burst into tears. 'I didn't really want to do it and I daren't tell anybody. And Dr Cavendish is so nice but if I tell him it will go on his notes and they'll be there for the rest of my life. Besides, he knows me and he's a friend and I—'

'You can tell me. I'm not a doctor, you're not my patient, I don't take notes. We're just two old school friends catching up.' Then Alice decided to take a chance. 'But I do have some medical knowledge.'

Ann dried her eyes, took a larger handkerchief out of

her bag and blew her nose. Her voice still quavered but she was trying to make it stronger. 'You know how you can love somebody and yet things just seem to go wrong?'

'I know,' said Alice. 'And especially when you're parted from each other.'

'Well, I do love Alec and I always have but…he was away and I was lonely…'

It was a sad story, Alice thought, but perhaps not uncommon. Ann had met a visitor to the island. He seemed nice, they had a brief one-night stand. Afterwards she felt guilty but later on she felt more guilty. And terrified. The signs were certain. She had been infected by some kind of sexually transmitted disease. 'And there's this pain in my sides all the time. What if I've got AIDS, Alice? What about the children?'

Alice managed to keep her expression neutral. 'No need to worry about that quite yet.' She thought for a moment. 'Did you say you were suffering from pain in your sides? Sort of lower in your body, pelvic inflammation, in fact?'

'Yes. It's a dull sort of pain but it seems to be there a lot.'

'Right. Look, do you mind if I examine you?'

Alice wasn't a doctor and knew she shouldn't be acting as one. But still…the chances were that, working in one of the most cosmopolitan areas of London, she'd probably had more experience of this kind of disease than Ben. So she took Ann into the treatment room and examined her. Then she fetched a swab, took a sample. 'I can do this for you now, but you will need further tests for other diseases. Just sit here and read a magazine for a minute. I'll fetch you a cup of tea and I'll be back in a while.'

It wasn't a kit that Alice used often. A home testing kit. She would much prefer to send samples to a large reputable laboratory and have the most definite diagnosis possible. But this kit was the latest state-of-the-art development and was guaranteed to be ninety-nine per cent successful.

Alice took the swab, followed the instructions. And then she sighed with relief. This was good news—of a sort. She went back to Ann. 'You've got chlamydia. It's nasty but if it's caught early then it's not too serious and I can get you the medicine to treat it sent in a plain envelope from the mainland. It can come here. It's an antibiotic. As I remember, it's doxycycline, a set of pills that you take for a week. And then you'll be cured.'

'You can do that for me? Alice, you're an angel. Oh, and you won't tell the doctor, will you? I couldn't bear him to know.'

Alice saw the hope drain from Ann's face as she didn't at once give the hoped for answer. But then she made up her mind. 'No, I won't tell the doctor. I do think you ought to, I know he'll be sympathetic. But I won't tell him. OK? In the meantime, I'll refer you to a genitourinary clinic on the mainland to be on the safe side.'

A much happier Ann had gone home and Alice waited for the phone call that she knew would come. And in time Ben did phone. His voice was hopeful. 'Alice? I saw Ann passing my window, she looked happy. Did you find out what was wrong?'

Alice hesitated, but this had to be said. 'Now you have to trust me. If there's a problem then I have dealt with it.'

Silence from the phone. Then, 'I'm Ann McCann's GP and I'm concerned about her.'

'I just told you, Ben. You have to trust me.'

There was another silence and then he said, 'Trust. That's a word that you've used a lot recently. You've felt that your trust has been abused. Well, I won't do that. Fair enough, I do trust you. And, Alice, thanks for your help.'

Alice put down the receiver. More and more she was realising that not all men were like Sean Evans. Ben wasn't. And she loved him for it.

Later that afternoon she went on another visit to one of the little settlements. Since she now lived over the job, she really enjoyed it when she had a reason—not an excuse—to go driving round the island. The women in the town had no difficulty walking to see her, but a fair proportion of the population lived in far-flung cottages and farms. There were no buses so people relied on their own transport. And if their husband needed the vehicle during the day…

She enjoyed her trip out, this was the furthest she had ever been. Near the town there tended to be visitors exploring their little bit of wilderness, but few of them got this far. Some distance from town she crossed a long section of boggy land, glad to use the four-wheel-drive. Often the surface of the road was covered with stagnant water, occasionally the water was deeper than she had realised. She didn't like it. Water belonged in streams and the sea, not on roads.

Eventually she came to the islet of Calvag. She stopped before crossing to it. Years ago she and Ben had cycled this far but they had decided to go no further than this. Careful or afraid? She wasn't sure which.

There was a shallow stretch of sea between the mainland and the island, and to get to the island it was necessary to drive across a fifty-yard causeway. The causeway had been built many years ago, now parts of it were crumbling. There was talk of European money being available to rebuild it but it hadn't appeared yet. At low tide the causeway stood proud of the water. At high tide the sea washed over it—but only deep enough to cover the bottom of a vehicle's tyres. In good weather, that was. In bad weather, things could be different.

Alice had checked the tides, knew that everything should be fine. And the sun was shining and the mountains stood clear. All would be well.

There was a little row of cottages, only four of them inhabited. She was visiting Eleanor Reay, a primigravida thirty weeks into her pregnancy. The usual pencilled notes told Alice that at the moment there was no husband with her. He was one of the many who had to work away—in his case, on the ferries. He got home for a longish stay once a fortnight and had arranged for time off when the birth was imminent.

It was Alice's first visit to Eleanor, she felt a little guilty at not having visited her so far. But Eleanor didn't mind, she was happy where she was. 'I get on well with the other people here, even though they are mostly a bit older than me.'

'You don't get lonely?'

Eleanor laughed. 'Well, soon I'll have a baby to keep me company, won't I? No, I don't get lonely. Did I hear that you used to work in London?'

'For the last fifteen years.'

Eleanor shook her head. 'I've only been once and I knew it wouldn't suit me. All the noise and the smell and so many people! There's just no peace there. And I like to live here because of what the land can give me. See those pictures?' She pointed to a set of pen-and-ink drawings of seabirds, lined neatly on one wall. Alice had noticed them when she'd come into the living room but hadn't liked to go over and look at them. Now she did. 'They're lovely,' she said, 'so precise.'

'I draw them and I sell quite a few. Drawing keeps me from being lonely.' From a drawer she took a large album. 'You know how a lot of people keep a set of photographs of their baby, showing how it's growing? Well, I'm going to do something different. I'm going to do a set of drawings. See, I've done the first one. Twenty weeks before birth.'

Alice had never seen anything like it. Eleanor had obviously worked from the ultrascan of her baby, taken at twenty weeks. But somehow she had taken the vague image and turned it into a living thing. There was love in the drawing. 'I think that's wonderful,' she said, and meant every word.

So far Eleanor was turning out to be the perfect mother-to-be. She was eating well, resting properly, keeping her body fit. She practised relaxation every day. She knew exactly what to expect, had read every book suggested to her. Only one thing to decide now.

Alice was hesitant. Eleanor was so obviously happy with her lonely home. It would be possible for her to come out here and deliver the baby but it would mean leaving her work for some time. That would make things difficult as there would be no one to take her place. 'Have you any thoughts about the delivery?'

Fortunately Eleanor was very practical. 'I'd love to have the baby here,' she said, 'but I realise that would be selfish. So will you book me into your new birthing unit?'

'Happy to,' said Alice gratefully. 'I'd like to stay here with you but…you're right. It would be difficult.'

Alice felt happy as she set off back. Eleanor was the perfect primigravida. She knew what to expect and was prepared for it. If only all mothers-to-be were like her!

The tide had turned when she re-crossed the causeway, the water higher. Alice smiled. She didn't mind. Perhaps she was getting over her irrational fear of water.

'This is Soalay weather,' Ben said next day. 'We know what to expect.' He was standing beside her outside the surgery, both were looking up at the mountains. They couldn't see the mountain peaks, which were shrouded in mist. And there was dampness in the wind that blew against them. 'It's going to rain.' He was stating the obvious.

They were standing by his Land Rover. Alice was in her uniform, of course, but she threw a set of heavy waterproofs and a pair of Wellingtons into the car. They could well be needed.

It was the afternoon and she was going out with Ben again. He was going to check on the progress of a woman who had a broken arm as there was some suggestion of infection. She also had a child who needed injections. Ben had suggested that this was her work so they could drive out together. It would be a good idea not to make their patients both come into town.

Alice had agreed that it would be a good idea. But she wondered because if he really did need her, he could have given the injections. Perhaps he just wanted her company? The thought made her feel warm inside.

'Fiona was asking when we'd see you again,' he said as they drove out of town. 'She's quite missing you.'

'I'm missing her. My flat is lovely and I'm very happy there but I remember staying at Taighean dhe Gaoithe and…'

Then she stopped. She couldn't really tell a man just how much she had enjoyed living with him in his house. It might seem a bit…forward.

This was the first time they'd been really alone together for any length of time since her cut-short dinner party. The first time they'd been alone since he had kissed her. Nothing had been said about it. She wondered if it had been just one isolated incident that was of no importance to him and would be quickly forgotten. She hadn't forgotten it. And she thought— hoped—that he hadn't either.

Today they drove to the opposite end of the island, the hillier end. And as they left the town, the expected rain started. Steady at first, but then a definite downpour, rattling on the windscreen and making it hard to see what was ahead. Ben switched on the lights. Alice decided not to say anything as he needed to concentrate. But it was a pity. She thought they needed to talk.

They reached the farmhouse that was their destination, managed to park right by the front door and then dash inside without bothering with their wet-weather clothes. And everything else went well. There was no problem with the broken arm, the little boy who needed the injections stood there and accepted them calmly, the household was happy and healthy. One quick mug of tea and they were on their way.

'Ahead of schedule,' he said, 'that's unusual.'

'In medicine, every job takes twice as long as the time allowed for it,' she quoted. 'But this was the exception that proved the rule. Did you know that in that saying, the word "proved" meant tested?'

He glanced at her, disconcerted. 'No, I didn't. But now the saying makes sense. Alice, did you know that you still have the power to surprise me?'

'Good,' she said.

If anything, the rain was even harder now and they were bumping slowly down a narrow road along the side of a narrow valley. And, as had happened so often recently, she remembered something. A flash of complete recollection, as if what had happened had happened yesterday, not sixteen years before.

'Stop here,' she said when they were halfway down the valley. 'Stop here, pull in by that big rock.'

He was shocked by the urgency of her tone.' Why? Are you all right? Not sick or anything?'

'I've never felt better. But pull in anyway.'

He did as she urged him and when they'd stopped she leapt out of the car, dashed for the shelter of the big rock. After a moment he joined her. The rock was undercut, they were standing, sheltered from the rain, in what was almost a cave. The rain hung like a silver curtain over the cave entrance.

They stood, silent, irresolute, looking at each other.

After a while he said, 'You have that look in your eye. I suspect that you have memories of this place.'

'Don't be shy with me, Benjamin Cavendish! You remember this rock very well! We came here when we were cycling together.'

'We covered most of this island while we were cycling. What was special about this place?'

But she knew by the half-smile on his face that he did remember. Her voice was dreamy as she said, 'I was just getting to know you. We'd come up here on our bikes and it started to rain. It wasn't raining like this, we knew it was only a shower so we came here to shelter. And then…'

'And then I kissed you,' he said. 'I had wanted to for so long.'

'And I had wanted you to kiss me. But I wasn't as forward then as I was now.' She looked at him expectantly.

'Give me a moment to catch up,' he said. He took her by the arms, pulled her closer to him. Then he kissed her—on the forehead.

Was that it? she wondered. What about two nights ago? There had been so much more passion then.

But then he had been in a hurry. They had more time now. He slid his arms round her but still held her only loosely. He kissed each cheek then but, still holding her, moved back a little. 'I love looking at your face,' he said. 'I see the young girl, the first girl I ever kissed with any real intent and I felt so much for her. Now I see not a girl but a woman, who is older but who is even more lovely than the girl—if that is possible.'

'That's a nice thing to say. Now you can kiss me properly.'

He did kiss her and it seemed to last for ever. And behind them the rain spattered on the bare rocks and they seemed locked in their own little world.

After a while their lips parted and they stood cheek to cheek and talked a while. Their bodies were still crushed together and she could feel the throbbing of his heart against her breasts. She could feel the equally wild throbbing of her own heart! What was he doing to her?

'So now what?' he asked, his voice tense. 'What do you want of me? This is so good—but I'm not sure that it's a very good idea.'

She didn't want to talk—she didn't want to think. All she wanted was for him to kiss her again and just to feel. Couldn't they wait just a few moments more before they had to enter the real hard world and talk? So she leaned forward and kissed him again. His arms tightened again round her. And, yes, they could wait a few moments more.

But in time the talking had to start. She had to answer his questions—*so now what*? And his other question—*what do you want of me*? She wasn't sure she knew the answer to either.

'I don't know what I want of you,' she said. 'I'm not sure what I want in general. This has happened three or four times since I got back here on Soalay and since I met you again. Memories jump back that are so real.'

She felt confused. 'And they're not like the memories of my parents or my schooldays or how I was happy enough. All my strongest memories are of you. I wonder if I'm trying to get back the feelings I had for you all those fifteen years ago.'

'We were young, we didn't know what we had. We didn't know how wonderful it was. I shouldn't have talked you into going to London. I let you go.'

'It was my decision!' she protested. 'I knew what I was doing.' Then there was a pause and she had to add, 'No, I didn't know what I was doing. I was going to train in Edinburgh so I could be near you, and then I got that offer from Royal Harriwells in London. I didn't expect it. But it was the best midwifery training school in Britain.'

'You had to take it. And I could have tried to find a place in London—but I didn't. So we parted. We promised to keep in touch but…'

It had been a long time ago but she remembered it so well. 'I suppose that what happened was inevitable,' she said. And both of them fell silent.

At first, of course, they had kept in touch. But for both of them there had been the excitement of living in a big city. And for both of them the demands of work had been hard. So perhaps it had been inevitable that they would drift apart. The letters, the phone calls had grown more infrequent. And eventually, after some months, an honest letter from Ben. He had met a girl on a course, was seeing something of her…he thought it right that Alice should know. She had replied kindly they had to get on with their lives, they could remain friends. But they had drifted even further apart. Letters had become more and more infrequent, after two years only Christmas cards. And then even they'd stopped.

'If we'd been together in Edinburgh then I might have married you instead of making the big mistake I did make. We could have come back to Soalay as we planned.'

This was dangerous talk, she had to put him right. 'No, Ben, no one knows what might have happened. Perhaps we needed time apart. But then you make a choice and you have to live with it—and with its consequences.'

'True.' His tone was morose.

She felt she had to go on. 'And there have been consequences. You've been hurt, I've been hurt. But you've got Fiona and you love your life here. I'm getting over what happened to me—but I don't want to be tied down. I'm here for respite for a year and then I'm going to carry on with my career in London. I'm going to be a high-flyer.'

'I can tell that,' he said. 'You've got the drive for it, you always did.'

'Things aren't the same,' she told him. 'They can't be. We've both got our paths to follow now and they're different.'

She paused. She half wondered, half hoped that he was going to contradict her. But he remained silent. So dolefully she said, 'Look, the rain's getting less. Perhaps we ought to go.'

'Have you remembered what you wanted to remember?'

'I have. But memories are in the past and we have to live in the present.'

But as they dashed back to the car she wondered if

all they were doing was trying to recapture the past. The past was memories, her feelings were of today. Then she had been an eighteen-year-old, unsure of the world and what she wanted from it. Now she was a mature woman and her feelings were vastly different from those of the child she had been. Now she was in love. Really in love. But she dared not say anything.

CHAPTER EIGHT

She didn't know then how much that was going to be a day to remember.

Ben came into her clinic with her, he needed to check the notes that had been made on a young boy some time ago. His mother had brought him in, declaring very loudly that the nurse had not given him his due injections three years before. Ben was not so sure.

While he was leafing through the notes Alice checked her messages. One made her frown—from Cara Garrett in Lonkille. Her husband was away. And two-year-old Hamish had gone down with a very bad cold—possibly even flu. Cara was worried—what should she do? Should she call out the doctor?

'This is partly for you,' Alice said when Ben came back to her room and played the message for him. 'My guess is that there's probably nothing wrong with him but I'd like to check. Cara seems to me to be a pretty sensible person. I'll phone her, tell her to put Hamish to bed with plenty of liquids and I'll drive out there later this evening. The rain might have stopped by then.'

'It won't have stopped, it's going to get worse.

Anyway, this is a call for me as much as for you. You call Cara and tell her that someone will come later, I'll go home and put Fiona to bed and then come back here to pick you up. Say, in a couple of hours?'

'There's really no need, Ben! I can cope quite well.' But secretly she was pleased that Ben wanted to come with her. She didn't fancy driving all that way through this torrential rain.

'As you say, it's likely to be as much my case as yours. See you in two hours.' And he was gone.

He seemed very keen on the trip, Alice thought as she watched his car drive out of the car park. Almost as if he wanted to spend time with her. But hadn't they just spent time together? And agreed that they were following different paths, that they had to live in the present? She thought it a bit odd.

However, when he came back to pick her up she was more than pleased. It seemed impossible but the weather had got worse. She had never experienced anything like this in London—and seldom here, in her childhood. The rattle of rain on the vehicle's roof was almost deafening, the rain was hitting the tarmac in front of them and bouncing upwards.

He drove cautiously as visibility was minimal. And the road was often covered with water. It got worse when they had to pass through the boggy section, Alice was glad that Ben was doing the driving. Of course, she could have coped. But she was happy that she didn't have to.

They arrived at Cara's house, the cottage looking decidedly woebegone in the rain. But all was well inside. Like so many medical callouts, the problem was the parent's anxiety rather than the patient's illness. Hamish did have a very bad cold, but rest, drink and infant paracetamol to lower his temperature were all that he really needed. Still, that's what you had to expect as a nurse or doctor.

The weather was just as bad on the way back. But because they were going home, Alice felt more relaxed. She chatted easily to Ben, sticking to subjects that interested them both but which weren't personal. Scottish independence, yes or no? They could debate that for hours.

She wondered if she should invite Ben in for a drink. She'd like him to come in but she still wasn't quite sure of his attitude to her. He had kissed her twice now—that was, kissed her twice as if it had meant something. And she was sure it had meant as much to him as it had to her. But to invite him in for a drink? Might he think that it was an invitation to something more? Did she *want* to invite him to something more? It was all rather difficult. And she was pleasantly tired.

They talked about the advantages of a dedicated birthing unit. Then they talked about the differences in work between that of a country GP and a city-centre GP. Ben, of course, thought that the country GP's work was more satisfying. Both were relaxed, enjoying themselves. Which was, of course, when things tended to happen.

The rain was as hard as ever but now the wind had grown. The Land Rover was buffeted, she could feel it rocking underneath her, but Ben drove on steadily. She decided she'd be glad to get home.

They came to a small bridge that crossed a stream at the edge of the marshlands. Ben slowed, drove carefully in the centre of the road. Suddenly the Land Rover skidded to the edge of the bridge, lurched sideways at what seemed an impossible angle. Alice looked downwards. She could see running water just below her. She screamed, they were going to drop into the river, she'd be trapped and she'd drown! Beside her she heard Ben curse, felt rather than saw him heave at the steering-wheel.

It couldn't have been long, perhaps a second. But to Alice it felt like a lifetime. The vehicle teetered on the edge, then the wheels got a grip and dragged it back onto the road.

Alice couldn't help it. Perhaps she was safe now but she sobbed as if her life was in danger.

Ben drew up a dozen yards down the road. He unfastened both their safety belts then pulled her to him. She heard his voice, no, she felt his voice—gentle, comforting, reassuring. 'Alice, you're all right. That was a bit exciting for a moment but you're all right now. You're safe. Alice, it's all right.'

She had to cling to him. There was comfort in the smell of his jacket, the strength of his arms round her. Slowly she came back to normal. She felt her heartbeat steady, stopped sniffing and lifted her head from his shoulder. He offered her a handkerchief. And then, just a bit, came shame. 'Sorry, I overreacted. I didn't mean to go on like that. It's just that I…'

'It's OK, there's nothing to worry about. I was scared myself—though the water there isn't very deep.'

He frowned. 'We'd better get you home. You must be tired, we'll get you back and you can have an early night.'

'I'm not tired! I was terrified! I've always been terrified since…since…'

And then he remembered. 'Of course! You were in an accident when you were twelve! I remember you telling me about it—your dad's car rolled into a stream. For a moment your head was under water and you've been terrified ever since.'

'I'm all right with water and I'm all right in cars. But if there's any chance of a car going into water then I just lose control. It's stupid I know but…'

'It's not stupid! It's a perfectly natural reaction. But now we're in no great hurry. I want you to sit here with me, lean against me. In a moment I'll put my arms round you and you must try to relax.' He took her hand, felt for her pulse. 'You're not over it yet, are you? But it's finished now and you're all right.'

Of course she knew what he was doing. The soft voice was hypnotic, he was reassuring her, telling her that all would be well, doing all the things, in fact, that she would do herself for someone suffering from shock. But it didn't matter that she knew what he was doing. She could feel it working. And there was something more, there was a touch of sincerity in his voice that convinced her that his care for her was genuine. Whatever it was, she liked it.

She just lay against him. He was big and strong and comforting and she wanted to stay here for ever. Just a minute! She was a medical professional herself! She had to be able to deal with emergencies. She sat upright, pulling away from him.

'Ben! We're not the only people to use this road.

Don't you think you ought to phone the police, tell them about the damage to the bridge? The next people along might not be as lucky as us.'

'Good point. I'll do it at once.' He felt in his pocket for his mobile and she listened to his incisive voice. 'Sergeant Cullen? Dr Cavendish. I'm by the bridge on the Bunness Road and there's a bit of a problem here. Half the bridge had broken away… The first bridge after the turning… Right.'

There was more conversation and then he turned to Alice and said, 'Sergeant Cullen will organise someone from the council to come at once and see what can be done—even if it's only closing the road. Now we will get you home.'

He came up to her flat with her. Alice looked at the clock and blinked. It was only nine p.m. 'It's been a long day,' she said.

'Would you like me to leave you alone or would you like some company for a few minutes? After you've had a shock, it's sometimes good to have someone around even if they don't do very much.'

'If you don't mind, I'd like you to stay for a while,' she said. 'But what about Fiona?'

'She's long since asleep and if she does wake up, Mrs McCann will see to her. How are you feeling now?'

How was she feeling? Better, much better. And somehow restless. 'I'm improving by the minute,' she told him. 'Why don't you pick some music while I make us some tea?'

She hurried into the kitchen to put the kettle on and

then went into her bedroom and changed out of her uniform into trousers and a big loose shirt. She remained barefoot. When she took the tray of tea and biscuits into her living room she found that he had chosen one of her favourite old collections to play—that was, one of their old favourites. Call her old-fashioned but she felt that there was no mood music like that of Frank Sinatra.

Ben was sitting on her couch. She put the tray in front of him on her coffee-table and sat by him. A conscious, deliberate decision. She sat by him, not opposite him. They both drank tea and then he took her wrist, felt her pulse. 'Still a bit fast and erratic,' he said. 'I thought it might have settled down by now.'

'Perhaps it will in time. But now let me take your pulse.'

He offered her his wrist, she wrapped her fingers round it. 'I think yours might be a bit fast too,' she said.

'But that near-accident didn't really bother me.'

'I think we've gone beyond the accident, haven't we?'

Somehow, she was no longer taking his pulse, she was holding his hand. And somehow their other hands were together too. Just holding hands. They sat there together with that the only contact, and for a while that was quite enough for her. For a while.

Then he leaned forward, wrapped his arms round her and gathered her to him. She felt calm, relaxed there, almost as if she were coming home. This was proper, this was what ought to be. For now this was where she belonged.

His kiss, when it came, was gentle, tentative, as if he wasn't quite sure of the reception he might get. But she loved it, and somehow he knew. She felt her body soften, relax even more, as if all worry had gone from it. Whatever happened, it would be right. Because he was Ben and they were in…no, she would not say it, would not even think it. For the moment there was only now.

She stroked the back of his neck, played with his hair, caressed the hands that held her. It was so good to lie here like this. But it could not go on like this for ever.

The kiss deepened, became more demanding, his arms held her more tightly. Perhaps she heard his breathing, perhaps it was his increasing heartbeat, she could feel it under the softness of her breasts. And suddenly she wasn't languorous any more. Excitement, anticipation throbbed through her. She was with Ben, she was his lover, not of fifteen years ago but a mature woman who knew what she needed and what she had to give. Giving! She needed to give to him.

He was Ben. She knew he was honest and fair and the last man on earth to take advantage of someone, especially of someone whom he… Well, someone he liked. So she was not surprised when he drew back. released her and took a deep shuddering breath. 'Alice, this is not good. We're both tired and we're likely to do something that we will regret.'

'It is good! You know it and so do I! Ben, this is no undertaking for the future. It is only now and I want exactly what you want. We're old friends—old lovers, in fact—and we know we can trust each other. So come back to me.'

Now they were sitting at opposite ends of her couch. She crossed her arms, took hold of the loose shirt and pulled it over her head. She threw it on the floor and said again, 'Come back to me.' And waited.

He moved towards her. His hand stretched out, a finger stroked down the side of her face, across her neck, ran across the swell of her breasts. It was a tiny caress. But her heart beat to the feel of it. And then he was with her again, arms wrapped round her, straining her body to his. She revelled in the passion that she had unleashed in him, knew now that there could be only one possible ending to their evening. The kiss seemed to go on for ever. And then they were no longer sitting on the couch but standing by it. Kissing still, of course, but she knew that now things must be different. She felt a last tremor of anxiety, of fear even, but it passed at once.

It wasn't like her. She had never been a coquette, never one to tease. But now was different. She stepped back from him, reached behind her and released the clip of her lacy white bra. Then she shook it from her shoulders. She linked her hands behind her neck and thrilled at his reaction, the desire that burned in his eyes as he saw the curve of arm, breast and waist.

'Come with me,' she said, and took him by the hand.

Her bedroom curtains were drawn, she flicked the switch of her bedside light and a dim yellow light cast shadows across the room.

She remembered his body from the past and felt a sudden urgency, a need to touch him, to press her hardened nipples against his chest. Ben's fingers were tugging at her belt and buttons, trembling with a sudden controlled urgency, his usual sureness lost to passion. He gently pushed her trousers down to her hips and lowered her onto the bed. She smiled at the determined expression on his face as he lowered his head to hers.

He kissed her neck, her closed eyes, framed her face with his strong hands, kissed and stroked her into what felt like heaven. Her skin felt on fire, alive, loved, the tension of the accident leaving her body to be replaced with a drugged heavy pleasure, the warmth spreading to all her body, transforming to that sweet ache between her thighs.

Alice felt a warmth and happiness that transcended anything she had felt before. She tingled with anticipation, she wanted him to kiss her breasts, she wanted… she wanted all of him. Cruelty. He had stopped, he was struggling to undo his belt. She wanted to be naked against all of him, needed to be close to his maleness and wanted that feeling of being both protected and threatened by his masculinity. She needed to feel his body heat and the intensity of his need. She smiled, an impish quirky smile, and momentary doubt flickered across his face as, taking him by surprise, she pushed him so that now he was underneath her. She felt that fleeting power women had before sweet capitulation. His eyes gleamed in the soft light, his want written on his face. He seemed oddly vulnerable, younger, and for a moment she saw the Ben of fifteen years ago, and felt a brief sadness that he was gone for ever.

His eyes slowly took in the lines of her body, the curve of her breast, the soft sweep of hair lying against creamy flesh and travelled down to the shadowed promise below. His shudder of frustration heightened her response.

She wanted to play, to delay that which she wanted more than anything else in the world. She offered her breast to his lips and arched with the pleasure he brought her. She brushed her breasts against his chest and felt his response. Alice knew neither of them could wait much longer. He sat back and she helped him remove the few garments he had left. Then both sighed with pleasure as he was free to lie against her, warm and damp against her belly, a promise and an exciting threat. She knelt over him again, her hair falling softly against his chest, kissing him and moving gently against him in that eternal accelerating rhythm, filled with an urgency she had never felt so intensely before.

Again she smiled at Ben, her eyes crinkling with mischief, wanting to again delay delight, needing to exercise her power over him, to test the depth of his passion. 'You witch, you're teasing me,' he said in a tender whisper, and effortlessly turned her over.

Now he was astride her body, his eyes drinking in the beauty of the lines of her breast, the golden down on her shapely arms, the inviting darkness between her thighs. He stroked the curve of her cheek, the dark intensity of her eyes echoing his feelings. He couldn't wait much longer, but he knew that this first time had to be right, he knew that it was important to her to explore and be explored, important for her to have this power of with-holding and then giving pleasure. He knew she would give all of herself without doubt or self-consciousness, her pleasure heightened by his.

He realised that pleasing her was as important as taking his own pleasure. Her body was at once familiar and new, his body remembering the intensity of the love-making of their youth. Suddenly he was a suppli-cant, pleading for her to open to him.

Alice had never wanted this as much as now, had never had such a desperate need to assuage the sweet ache, never felt the pain of such intense need before. She felt as if there had been no one else, she felt she was a novice at loving like this. She sensed the change in Ben and revelled in her capitulation, 'Now,' she said. 'Please, now.' Taking him in her hands until he gave an inarticu-late cry, pulled her hands over her head and entered her. All reason was gone. Sensation replaced thought as their bodies joined in the timeless accelerating rhythm of love.

She would have liked to stay there in bed for ever. Lying on her back, her head on her arm, his hand stroking her cooling body. Something struck her and she giggled. 'You organised the furniture for this flat, didn't you?'

'Did the best I could,' he muttered. 'I worked on the same principle that I use when I buy presents. Always get something that you really like yourself. Then you know that at least one person is going to be happy with your choice.'

'Well, I think you did very well. But just one question. If you bought furniture for a single-person flat, why did you order a double bed?'

'That's a good question. And I don't know the answer. I certainly wasn't expecting anything like this.'

'Well, I'm glad you did get a double bed. I like it.'

She rolled over and kissed him on the cheek. 'Now I'm just going to lie here for five minutes and then we jump back into the real world.'

'Five minutes,' he said, and in his turn rolled over to kiss her bare shoulder. 'Five wonderful minutes.'

She closed her eyes. Just five minutes of thinking nothing but that she was so blissfully happy. It wasn't very long but she knew that it was all that they could spare.

Her time was soon over. Showing more strength than she'd known she possessed, she sat up, pulled the sheet over her breasts. 'You have to go,' she said. 'You have a daughter at home and you have to work tomorrow.'

He sat up too, took her hand in his. 'I suppose so. Alice, that was so wonderful.'

She nodded dolefully. 'It was. And you know it's been hanging over us both since we met again. I've been thinking about what we did all those years ago, wondering if it would still be so marvellous and if—'

'It was still so marvellous!' There was a pause and then he said. 'But now what?'

This was the crux of the matter and she knew she had to be resolute. 'Now nothing. We both know we can't have a future. You're still hurting after your divorce, I'm still hurting after my break-up and the mess at the hospital. I'm even scared of you, thinking that you could hurt me even more than Sean did. Yes, what we've just had was wonderful but it can't go on. And we have to work together. That would make it harder.'

Silence for another minute and then when he spoke his voice was sombre. 'I suppose you're right. We're not teenagers any more. It would be nice to think that we're older and wiser. And we mustn't do this again, it could become addictive.'

There was nothing she could say. She knew he was

right, but…but she had to accept it. 'Kiss me one more time and then get dressed and go,' she whispered. 'Let's part while all is good between us.'

He did kiss her. But it wasn't the kind of kiss that it had been before. She lay still in bed and watched as he pulled his clothes on. Another swift kiss on the forehead and he was gone. She thought that perhaps he was right. If he had to go it was best that he go quickly.

Alice lay back on her pillow and tried to work out whether she was happy or sad. Happy first of all—their love-making had been all and more than she had expected. She could lie here in bed for ever, a small smile on her face, just thinking about it.

Sad? What about the future? She had felt that she had to offer him a way out, make him feel that he was under no obligation to her. But when she had said that they couldn't go on, he could have contradicted her, couldn't he? Could have said at least that…could have said what? She wasn't sure what she wanted.

Was she trying to persuade herself that making love with Ben had been a single experience, a one-off, not to be repeated? Almost therapy, in fact? Now she wasn't very sure. But it had been so wonderful. So she slept.

Ben didn't want to go straight home. He knew he'd find happiness there, just gazing at the face of his sleeping daughter. But before that he needed to understand his feelings, to make sense of the whirling thoughts that were troubling him, to resolve the conflict that he felt. So he turned off the road, bumped down a farm track, and eventually parked on cliffs overlooking the sea. He sat, listening to faint murmur of waves below. It soothed him—a little.

What to do about Alice? Making love to her had brought back all the emotions he had felt so many years before. Could he still love someone after fifteen years apart? Right now he felt he could. But…she wasn't a girl now but a career-woman. If he was in love then he was in love with the present Alice, not the memory of the past. However, she had set her heart on going back to London in a year's time, taking up this new job. Soalay was just a place for rest and recuperation.

He had been married and it had been a disaster. Why risk disaster again? But now he felt lucky—out of it he had got Fiona and she was the centre of his life. Could her risk Fiona's happiness in any way?

Did he have a choice? When he'd left, Alice had been quite definite. He remembered her words when they had talked about this. Now nothing. We both know we can't have a future. Well, that had been clear enough.

He knew what he had to do—nothing. Carry on with Alice as a friend and a colleague and feel sorry when she left at the end of her year. Pretending that they meant so little to each other was a pretence, but they could both keep it up. But then he remembered their love-making. It would be so hard to give up that—but he would have to.

Alice wasn't sure how she would face him next day. Or how he would want to face her. He had his surgery, she had her clinics. They could try to keep apart but they were in adjoining buildings and their paths crossed constantly. Often they had coffee together. She just didn't know what would happen.

In fact, he came over to see her at lunchtime, asking to see the patient notes of a child. They looked at each other as she handed the notes over, her receptionist hovering in the background.

'I've had a phone call from the police,' he said, 'thanking us for letting them know about the bridge. The local works department is mending it now, but things could have been very nasty.'

'Very nasty,' she agreed. 'But now everything is all right.'

'I'm sure it is.'

She thought she could see the relief in his eyes and she felt sad as she heard the unspoken message. Last night had happened. It had been wonderful but it wasn't to be spoken of again. And it certainly wasn't to happen again. They would still be friends and carry on as before.

She was now working hard and really enjoying it. Her circle of friends was enlarging. There were a surprising number of people who remembered her, and she felt she was becoming part of island life again. She was asked to give a talk to the local women's group and she talked about the concept of a birthing unit, invited the group to have a tour.

Afterwards she was invited to join the group. She said she would—but time was always a problem. Now she felt she was part of a living community, something she had never felt in London.

She still saw a lot of Ben but their relationship was now

more complex. When they met there was now a bond between them that was felt but unspoken. She saw it in his eyes, heard it in apparently casual conversation. They had fused together in a way that could never be forgotten.

But this bond was going nowhere. Neither knew where they were going, both were too afraid to try to push things further. She had thought of inviting him for a meal again—but she always backed away from the idea. It would seem too much like a challenge. Perhaps twice a week she called in at Taighean dhe Gaoithe to see Fiona—but she tried to do it when she knew Ben wouldn't be there. Mrs McCann was always pleased to see her. So life was carrying on.

But there was always the feeling that all was not settled between her and Ben. They had unfinished business— though how it was going to finish she didn't know. Some decision had to be made but no way could it come from her. Whatever it was, it had to come from him.

When it did come it came as a shock.

She had finished her afternoon's work by booking in two giggling women who had just discovered that they were really, truly pregnant. Now she was expecting to do a couple of hours of paperwork—she needed to order more stock. So far an ordinary, quite pleasant day.

Her phone rang. Not the official midwife and nurse's phone but her personal mobile. Only a few people knew its number but when she was out of her clinic she had urgent messages forwarded to it. At first she didn't recognise the voice. A woman obviously, but the accent was thicker than normal and the woman was obviously very upset. 'Alice, you've got to come at once! She's hurt, I think it's badly, and I've phoned the doctor but he's at the far side of the island and can't get back.'

Then Alice realised who it was. Mrs McCann. Then who could be hurt? There was only one possible person. Fiona!

Somehow she managed to quell her natural panic, tried to act like a medical professional. She made her voice sound confident, reassuring. 'Mrs McCann! Now, calm down, this is important but I'm sure we can sort things out. It's Fiona, isn't it? What exactly has happened to her?'

Mrs McCann reacted well to Alice's composed voice. 'Yes, it is the wee girl. She was playing outside and running along that garden wall. She fell off. I saw her but I couldn't stop her, and it's her leg. I think it's broken. She started screaming and I brought her inside and—'

'Is there any bleeding?'

'No. But her leg's all twisted and bruised looking. There a big swelling and I—'

'Don't try to do anything. Try to calm her, keep her lying down, try to stop her moving and cover her with something warm. I'll be there in a quarter of an hour. Did you say that you'd phoned Ben?'

'I did. He's away at the far side of the island, it'll take him at least an hour for him to come straight back. He said to phone you.'

Even though all her thoughts were on the emergency, Alice felt a tiny touch of pleasure at the thought that Ben should turn to her first. But she had work to do!

Her Land Rover was outside, she didn't need to

collect any medical supplies. There was always a full kit in the car boot. She shouted a quick word of explanation to Morag and then set off for Taighean dhe Gaoithe.

She was a professional, she thought as she drove, and forced herself to keep down to a safe speed. She had to think of Fiona as an A and E case, not a little girl she had come to love. Now, what did she remember about broken legs? It was hard, trying to detach herself from her feelings, but she had to do it. And what made it worse was that outside it was a lovely day—just the kind of day to sit in the sun and play with a little girl.

She skidded to a stop outside the house, grabbed the two cases that she thought might be of most use and ran to the open front door. 'Mrs McCann,' she shouted.

'Here. In the living room. We're here.'

The living room. Where so often she had sat companionably with Ben and watched the sun go down. But now there was a small form covered with a red blanket stretched out on one of the couches. There was the sound of a child sobbing and Mrs McCann's gentle voice. 'Now, then, my darling. Auntie Alice is here and soon everything will be all right.'

I hope so, Alice thought. She leaned over the little girl, kissed the tear-streaked face. 'We'll soon have you feeling better, darling,' she whispered. 'Now, just let Auntie Alice have a look at you.'

It wrenched at her heart to see Fiona's fear and pain. But love and sympathy weren't enough. She needed to be professional.

First, something to ease the pain. Well, that was easy

enough—she had powerful analgesics in her bag. An injection and after a minute Fiona's sobs diminished. Now the examination. It had been drummed into her in A and E that there might be an obvious injury that needed prompt treatment. But always check to see that there was nothing else wrong. With Mrs McCann's help Alice slid off Fiona's few clothes. A graze on one elbow but that was all. The only serious injury was the leg—but that was bad enough.

The leg was twisted and swollen but fortunately there was no bone protruding through the skin. Alice ran her hands gently over the site and winced. It felt like a complicated fracture—there was damage to the soft tissues around the break. This could be just as serious as the break itself. And Fiona was still young, at an age when bones could heal themselves more easily. But the damage to the soft tissues was bad.

Alice took one of Fiona's tiny toes, pinched the nail. The nail went white—but when Alice released it, did not promptly turn pink again. Poor capillary return. Blood wasn't circulating as it should, presumably because of an obstruction caused by the break. There was bleeding into the tissues. Alice grimaced. If the poor capillary return remained, it wasn't impossible that Fiona might lose her leg.

She had to do something! But this was not an A and E department with skilled staff, the battery of monitoring machines that kept constant vigilance over a patient's state. There was just Mrs McCann and herself. She didn't even dare wait for Ben to return. So Mrs McCann and she would have to manage.

'We're going to have to reduce the fracture,' she told the older lady. 'That means we have to pull the injured leg and straighten it. Then we have to tie the two legs together so that the whole one acts as a splint for the injured one. I can't do it on my own. You'll have to help me.'

Mrs McCann looked worried. 'Shouldn't we wait for the doctor?'

'I'd love to. But this is an emergency. It's what he'd want us to do.'

Alice settled her patient on her back and then moved to the end of the couch, by Fiona's feet. 'Hold her shoulders,' she told Mrs McCann. 'Hold them gently but firmly.' Then she took hold of the injured leg.

It took a while but she did it. She had no splint but once the legs were in position, she tied them together with bandages. It seemed to be a competent job. When pinched, the toe nail now showed instant capillary return. The immediate crisis was over.

Alice sat back, wiped her face with her handkerchief. She had managed. But it was the kind of job she never wanted to do again. She took one of Fiona's hands, held it.

It didn't seem long before she heard the sound of a car racing up the drive, the bang of the front door, footsteps running down the corridor. 'In the living room, Ben,' she called.

Ben rushed into the room, bent over to look at the sleeping Fiona. Alice could tell that he was distraught but had to admire his strength and self-control as he turned to her and asked, 'How have things been, Alice?' Good. For a moment they could be doctor and nurse.

She gave her report as clinically as she would have in a hospital A and E department.

He listened to her and then examined Fiona, apparently just as detached as he would be if he was in the same department.

Fiona marvelled at his self-control, thought that it was almost inhuman. Then she saw the way his hands were trembling, and she understood.

'I think you've done a great job, Alice. I couldn't have done anything more myself.' Then he became a father, not a doctor. Now his voice was shaking and in his eyes Alice could see the glint of tears. He bent over, kissed his daughter, stroked her pale forehead.

There was a tap on the door and Mrs McCann came in. When had she left? Alice wondered. She hadn't even noticed. And Mrs McCann was in tears herself. 'Is she all right, Dr Cavendish? It was all my fault. I should have been watching her and I—'

'It wasn't your fault, Mrs McCann. Accidents happen, especially to children. You ask Alice here. We just have to hope that all will be well. You did a great job. Alice has been telling me that she couldn't have managed without you. I hope you know how important your contribution was.'

'I just sat there and held her.'

'That was what was needed. Now, something more you can do for us. A couple of mugs of tea?'

'Right!' Mrs McCann set off back to her kitchen, obviously feeling that things were now better.

He turned to Alice. 'It was good of you to come out so quickly.'

'Ben! Don't be silly! I'd come for anyone, but especially for Fiona.' The words had to slip out. 'I love her, Ben.'

'So do I. God, how I love her.' He shook his head, horror showing in his face. 'For a while I thought there was the vague chance that I might lose her. And the very idea. I just couldn't cope.'

'But you haven't lost her, she's going to be all right. What was it like, driving across the island after Mrs McCann phoned you?'

'I can't remember much of the journey. All I knew was that I had to get here. Then I thought that you would probably be here and that calmed me just a little.'

The door opened and Mrs McCann brought in their two mugs of tea. There was also a large plate of buttered scones. 'How did you manage this so quickly?' Alice asked, waving at the scones.

'Thought you might like something to keep your strength up,' Mrs McCann said, before disappearing.

Alice had thought she wasn't hungry then she took the first mouthful of scone and discovered she was ravenous. Ben was the same.

When they had demolished the pile of scones, Ben said, 'This is another lesson for me. Or it's the same message I learned from my ex-wife Melissa. It's a mistake to love anyone too much. It's so easy to lose them. I've got Fiona, of course, but now I know it's just her and me against the world.'

Where does that leave me? Alice wondered. Two against the world—couldn't that be three? But she didn't say anything.

* * *

Ben took the next day off work and took Fiona on the ferry to the mainland. He'd arranged an appointment at the nearest hospital. The paediatric orthopaedic consultant said that Fiona had been very well treated and he saw no reason why she should not make a complete recovery. Ben phoned the news to Alice immediately and told her how complimentary the consultant had been about her reducing the fracture.

'That's good to know,' Alice said. 'Ben, I've got a suggestion. When you come back tonight, why not leave Fiona in my clinic for a few days? There's plenty of room and you know that Mrs McCann needs a bit of a rest. She'd only fret if Fiona was left with her.'

'Great idea! But it's more work for you. Sure you don't mind?'

'I'm certain I don't mind,' Alice said. Only when he had rung off did she wonder exactly why she wanted Fiona to stay. Certainly she thought it would be good for the little girl. But she knew that Ben would be in and out of her clinic. She'd see a lot of him.

And that was what happened. Fiona loved it in the clinic. She had no end of visits and Ben was always popping in. Alice liked this, too, though she knew that Ben was coming in to see his daughter and not her. She could accept that, it was fair. Still, he always stopped for a chat with her when he called.

Perhaps she should invite him for dinner again?

After four days Fiona was moved back to Mrs McCann's care. The day after that Ben brought her some flowers to say thank you from him and Fiona. Roses this time. And he gave her an invitation. 'Would you like to come with me on a social visit this evening?' he asked. 'Well, half social, half professional. You social, me professional. Sort of.'

'Social visit? Who to? Where? I'm intrigued.' She was also rather pleased. A social evening with Ben.

'I want to surprise you. Pick you up about seven?' So it was arranged.

She decided not to dress in her uniform but in something a little more fetching. She picked a pink summer dress and white sandals. She knew the outfit did a lot for her. She was looking forward to her surprise.

He picked her up punctually, drove her to a village about ten miles away. He parked, picked up a large bunch of flowers from the back seat and asked her to hold them. 'Not for you, I'm afraid,' he said, 'but I'd like you to give them.'

'I might have bought flowers myself if I'd known where we were going,' she said, slightly nettled.

'Sorry.' He grinned, obviously not sorry at all. 'And I'm afraid the flowers are from you, not me. I'm the professional, you're the guest. Smell them—aren't they something else?'

She did smell them and they were something else.

The were parked outside a tiny whitewashed cottage. It had an attractive pebbled front, with plants in pots and a garden seat. Ben knocked and Alice at once recognised who opened the door. Miss Morven!

She was now an old lady. Her once jet-black hair was now grey, but carefully cut. She wore a smart matching grey dress. She was also wore sunglasses, which rather surprised Alice. Sunglasses inside a house? It seemed to be an affectation that wasn't typical. Miss Morven had been her and Ben's primary-school teacher and she had always seemed full of common sense.

Miss Morven smiled at them, her head cocked slightly to one side.

'It's Ben Cavendish,' Ben said, 'and I've brought another of your ex-pupils to say hello.' Why did Ben have to introduce himself? Surely Miss Morven could… Then it all fell into place. Alice felt great sadness, a sense of desolation. Head cocked, dark glasses, Ben introducing himself? Miss Morven was blind.

'Lovely of you to come to see me, Ben. And this is?'

'You won't remember me, Miss Morven, but I was in your class.'

'Of course I remember you. It's Alice…Alice Muir. Come on in, dear, I've heard great things about you since you left. Midwife and children's nurse? You're certainly doing well. Ben told me all about you.'

They walked into the living room, Alice still slightly shocked. 'These flowers are for you,' she said, offering them.

Miss Morven reached out, felt for them and took them. Then she smelled them. 'They're lovely. There's roses…and lilies…and night-flowering stock. I can tell them all.' After smelling them, Miss Morven ran her fingers from blossom to blossom, caressing each flower with the lightest of touches.

For some reason that made Alice feel sad. 'Would you like me to put them in water for you?' she asked.

There was a hint of the teacher Miss Morven had

been in her reply. 'I'm blind, not helpless, Alice. I'll take the flowers and I'll make us all some tea. You can stop a while?'

'Alice is here as a visitor,' Ben said. 'But I'm here as a friend and a doctor as well. I've got a call to make in a house two streets away and I thought I'd have a look at you at the same time.'

'I'd phone if I was really ill,' Miss Morven said reprovingly. 'But it's kind of you to call. Now, sit down while I see to these flowers and fetch the tea.'

Alice sat, then looked around the room they were in. An ordinary, pleasant living room, no different from any other, scrupulously clean. There was even a television set. The only sign of Miss Morven's ailment was a white stick in the umbrella stand.

Miss Morven brought the tea in on a tray, placed it carefully on an occasional table. She sat and poured it out, handed cups to Alice and Ben. Then there were small plates with a napkin on each and carefully sliced cake. Alice had to smile. Miss Morven had always been exact, precise in her movements. And neat! Alice doubted that there had ever been a single pupil who had left Miss Morven's class without having the value of neatness instilled in them.

'You seem very comfortable here, Miss Morven,' Alice said.

'I am indeed. Now, do you take sugar? Then tell me about this new idea you're bringing to Soalay. What is a birthing unit?'

They chatted a while about old pupils and then Ben took Miss Morven into her bedroom. 'Just a quick check-up,' he said, 'and then I must go and see my other patient.' They came back into the living room ten minutes later and Ben told Alice that Miss Morven was as fit as a woman half her age. Miss Morven obviously thought this a compliment—but one that was deserved.

Ben took up his doctor's bag. 'I'll be back in fifteen minutes,' he said. 'You two chat till I come back.' Then he was gone and Miss Morven and Alice were alone.

'Tell me what it's like, coming back to the island after fifteen years,' Miss Morven said.

It was a question Alice had been asked often. And she often pondered on the changes, wondered if they were all for the better.

'Well, I've met a lot of old school friends,' she said. 'And most of them seem to have had babies. It makes me feel that I'm missing something.'

'Plenty of time yet,' Miss Morven consoled.

'There's more money about, more willingness to look to a future knowing that they have one here. The island is coming alive. Not as many have left as I thought would leave, and quite a few have come back to stay. Like Ben.'

'And like you.'

'Not me.' Alice thought it important to emphasise this point. 'I'm here for a year and then it's back to London. Perhaps I'll come back for the occasional holiday.'

'Of course. But we will see. You used to be very close to Ben, didn't you? I knew you were both children but I thought…there was something there that would be lasting. And there still is, isn't there?'

'No. You're wrong. There's nothing between Ben and me.' She hadn't intended it to happen but Alice's answer came out with more force than she had intended. She waited a moment and then said, 'Sorry. I didn't mean to be rude.'

'You weren't being rude, dear, you were making yourself clear. And I like that. Still…'

Miss Morven rose and walked confidently to an old dresser, took a thick book from a drawer. She offered it to Alice. 'I kept a record of all my classes,' she said. 'You and Ben are on page twenty-nine.'

Alice leafed through the book. Yes, there was her class, standing proudly on the steps of their tiny school. And there she was and there was Ben. Both were recognisable. And they both looked hopeful and untouched by life.

Silently, she handed the book back to Miss Morven.

'You know,' Miss Morven said conversationally, 'it's odd, I don't really find being blind is a handicap. You lose your sight but your other senses become more acute. I can hear far more than people realise they are saying. And I can hear and I can feel the relationship between you and Ben Cavendish.'

Alice had to ask. 'What can you feel? Ben and I are doctor and nurse and otherwise just good friends.'

'You know very well what I can feel,' Miss Morven said, shaking her head. 'You just have to admit it to yourselves. Now, would you like more tea and another slice of cake? I made the cake myself.'

'You're quiet, aren't you?' Ben said as they drove home. 'You chatted no end on the way out. Is Miss Morven being blind upsetting you?'

'Not really. I might have guessed that Miss Morven was tough, that she'd take everything that fate handed her.'

Then she spoke without really thinking of the consequences, perhaps not a good idea. 'She said something odd, Ben. She said that because she was blind her other senses had become more acute. She said that she could detect some…feeling between us. Some kind of special relationship.'

Ben shook his head. 'Just nonsense. She remembered how close we used to be. But we've grown up since then. We're good friends, I hope. But that is all. And, after all, you're leaving at the end of the year. Going back to take up that post in London.'

'I certainly am,' Alice said after a pause. She wondered if Ben really meant what he had just said. That Miss Morven's feeling that there was a special relationship between them was just nonsense. Did he really have to sound so certain?

CHAPTER NINE

THEY worked very well together. And when they were together they enjoyed each other's company. He seemed to need to see her quite often. Queries that could probably have been answered over the phone—he came to see her in person.

Sometimes, when he thought she wasn't noticing, she caught him looking at her, and she couldn't make out his expression. Whether it was sad or thoughtful she didn't know. But there was certainly some emotion there that he couldn't bring himself to express. He couldn't bring himself to admit what she was certain that he felt.

Once or twice she wondered if something should come from her, if she should be the one to speak first. She even considered trying by some means to get him into her bed again. Then she could show him what they meant to each other. But, of course, she couldn't. There were some steps that were too far. And imagine the feelings if he rejected her! They were too painful to contemplate.

No, Ben had to make the first move. She knew her feelings had improved no end—Ben had been largely re-

sponsible for that. Her fear and mistrust of men had now
almost gone. They were not all the same underneath!
But the remnants of the shadow of Sean still hung over
her. Any first declaration would have to come from Ben.

She loved him! And she was almost certain that he
loved her. Miss Morven had been entirely right. But
still he had to declare it. Even just talking about his
feelings would do. It would give her a chance to show
what she felt.

It was hard. When Ben touched her by accident, Alice
felt a thrill of excitement. It might be an arm round her
back as she got out of his car or a hand resting just a
second too long on her arm. And what made it harder was
that sometimes she felt he was doing it on purpose. As
if he couldn't bear to let her move away from his touch.

When she visited him at his home she always kissed
Fiona goodnight. Then later, when she left, sometimes
Ben would kiss her goodnight. But they weren't real
kisses. Just pecks on the cheek such as he might give to
anyone. How she wanted to throw her arms round him,
instead of resting them lightly on his shoulders, wanted to
turn her head so that he could feel her lips against his, her
mouth opening under his, feel the full force of her passion.

Of their passion! There was so little sign of it. She
was in love with Ben, but they were getting nowhere.

The crisis came a week later. She always had plenty
of mail—most of it junk, to be thrown straight into the
bin. But it still had to be sorted. Usually she went
through it at her morning coffee-break.

She was on her own, happy in her work, enjoying her
morning coffee. And there was a letter from the trust.

Technically her employer. Interesting. It looked an important letter.

Curious, she opened it, read through what it had to say, at first casually and then with increasing…increasing what? Alarm? Or excitement?

The secretary of the trust had written to her to say that the midwife whom Alice was replacing for a year had informed them that she would not be coming back to work. So a permanent job on the island was now vacant. The board felt that having three midwives in just over a year would not be a good thing and so they intended to advertise for a permanent candidate at once. A permanent candidate for her own job? Alice thought. But the letter went on to explain that, of course, when the permanent candidate took over her job, Alice would be relocated to another post for the rest of her contracted year. They had a post in mind for her. It would be a profitable move, there would be better conditions and an increase in salary.

Hands shaking, Alice put down the letter and poured herself another cup of coffee. She couldn't believe what she was reading. Her life was being turned upside down, being wrecked. She was happy here, happier than she'd thought she could be. How could they do this to her?

She started to read again. The secretary said that it was a legal requirement that the full-time job on Soalay be advertised. However, if Alice chose to apply for the position then the secretary felt certain that the board would look favourably on her application. They knew she was doing an excellent job.

Alice saw through the cautious wording. The trust

wanted her for the permanent job here—it was hers if she wanted it. Did she?

For the rest of the morning she wasn't sure what she did with herself. She had a visit to make, a clinic to run— and somehow she managed on autopilot. The question beat at her. What was she to do? Now she realised that she had been avoiding thinking about the future. She had been happy in her work, happy being close to Ben and Fiona, happy that her future was planned—she was leaving in a year's time. But a year was a long time. There was no need to decide anything yet. She could change her mind. Or someone could change her mind for her.

Now she had been forced into a decision after less than two months. And she wasn't ready yet! Did she want to stay or not? She had to make up her mind.

Perhaps it was a good thing but there was no chance of seeing Ben that day. He was spending the day giving a series of talks to the local school. But she knew when he was finishing, and when she knew he'd be free, she phoned him.

'Ben, I've got a problem, May I come over and talk to you later?'

'Of course you can.' She could hear the concern in his voice and love for him flared inside her for a moment. He went on, 'Anything serious? Anything I should know about now? Is it one of your or my patients?'

'It's not a patient. I don't want to talk over the phone, it's personal and I think we ought to be face to face.'

He paused before answering and there was a change in his tone when he spoke again. He sounded wary. 'Personal? OK, Alice. Would you like to come to tea with me and Fiona? Just something simple, I'm cooking. Mrs McCann is out for the evening.'

'No. I'd like to come to see you when Fiona's in bed. I've…got things to do before then. Well, things to consider.'

Another pause. 'Right, then. I'll see you when I see you.' He rang off.

She hadn't handled that very well, she thought.

She was going out to visit him only for an hour or so…she supposed. But she wanted to look her best. She felt that looking smart would add to her confidence— but what she had to be confident about, she didn't know. Still, she put on dark trousers, a vaguely see-through blouse, a matching blue jacket that she knew suited her colouring. She read through the letter again, tucked it into her pocket and set off.

As she drove to Taighean dhe Gaoithe she remembered when she had come to stay with Ben. How she had been both shy and slightly frightened—but still wondering what her stay there might bring. Only a handful of weeks ago. How things had changed!

She looked at the colours of moors, sea and sky. She thought of them as quiet colours—if colours could have a noise. But the colours had grown on her. This land was her birthright, she wanted to stay here.

But how could she stay? Not on her own, that was certain. Her life had been half destroyed by Sean. She felt she had regained much of her former strength, but she wasn't having it half destroyed again by another man who… What did he want?

She drove to the front of Taighean dhe Gaoithe, braking harder than usual and rattling the pebbles. Obviously Ben had been waiting for her as he appeared out of the front door at once. She felt that little jerk of excitement that always came when she saw him again. Even though it had been less than twenty-four hours since she'd seen him last. What was he doing to her?

As always, he had changed from his formal medical outfit and was now in a dark T-shirt and light chinos. He looked a picture of relaxation, looked wonderfully masculine and entirely... Stop it!

'Alice? Is everything all right? I felt a bit worried after your call.'

His obvious concern only made things worse. But she managed a smile—although a brittle one—and said, 'I've got a letter to show you. I need advice, I'm not sure what to do.'

Then a sudden terrible thought struck her. 'You didn't know about this, did you? Didn't know and didn't tell me—didn't warn me? That would have been a betrayal!'

Mildly, he said, 'Since I don't know what's in the letter, I can't tell you. But I can say that I've not had any letter about you recently and nothing would make me betray you in any way. Come on in, we'll have a drink and you can tell me all about it.'

I'm still not handling this well, she thought again.

She followed him into the living room, sat where she could look out to sea. She accepted the whisky and water that he brought her, sat there and tried to calm herself.

'There's no hurry,' Ben said. 'Take your time. I can see that you're upset.'

He sat opposite her. For a moment she thought that he might sit next to her, reach out and stroke her hair. He had done it once or twice in the past. But he didn't. Perhaps that was a good thing. She needed to be…not detached but neutral for a while.

When she felt she was calm she took out the letter and handed it to him. 'I received this this morning,' she said. 'I'm not sure what to do about it.'

She watched him read the letter, frown and then read it again. 'It's a fair letter,' he said after a moment. 'I can understand the trust's point of view, not wanting to change midwives three times in a year. And obviously they are trying to be very fair to you. There's a big hint that the job is yours if you want it.'

'So what do you think I should do?'

He sighed. 'Well, I think that you're a great midwife and children's nurse, you've made a big impression here. We'd all be very sad to see you go. But you have your career to think of, and what the trust has offered would be a step upwards.'

'So you think I should consider going in the interests of my career? Not consider applying for the full-time job here?'

He looked uncomfortable. 'Alice, since you came here you've been insisting that this was only a temporary job. A chance to get your breath back, to recover from what was obviously a very painful experience. Didn't you mean it?'

'Oh, I meant it.'

She sipped her whisky, hoped that he wouldn't notice her trembling hand. There was just one more thing she could say and still hold onto her dignity. 'Of course, you're right. I only came here as a temporary measure. There isn't really anything to keep me in Soalay, is there? I could easily leave at the end of the month.'

Her last hope. Now was when he could say that she had to stay, Soalay was now her home. He and Fiona needed her—there was no need of promises or plans for the future, just that she had to stay. She realised that this was why she had come, to hear those words.

But she didn't hear them. There was a long pause. 'We'd all be very sorry to see you go. But if you have to…'

So that was that. Her hopes, dreams, all smashed. In a remarkably casual voice she said, 'So that's settled. I'll write this evening and say I'm willing to leave Soalay as quickly as the trust wants me to.'

When Ben spoke his voice was hoarse. 'It's not my place to offer advice, but I'd like to suggest that you don't write at once. Wait a while. Give it a couple of weeks—that's the time they've given you. Who knows what might happen to make you change your mind?'

'I don't think anything will happen to make me change my mind,' she said, 'but, yes, I'll do as you say.'

She stood. 'No need to see me out, Ben. I know the way. I'll just pop my head round Fiona's bedroom door to look at her.' And she left him, closing the living room door on him.

Ben sat motionless in his chair, listening. He heard Alice's footsteps, could trace where they went to Fiona's bedroom, could imagine the door opening, perhaps even heard it creak. Silence for a moment and he pictured her leaning over the little bed, knew that she would straighten the bedclothes, kiss his daughter on the forehead. Then more footsteps, the click of the front door closing. And an over-revved engine and the crunch of gravel as she drove away.

He sighed. A desolate thought struck him—this could have been the last time Alice ever visited Taighean dhe Gaoithe. After so many happy times—what a memory she must take away!

He reached for the whisky bottle, poured himself a generous measure. He took a sip—and then poured half the contents of the glass back into the bottle. No problem was ever eased by drinking too much. He had seen too many patients who thought that it could.

He knew why Alice had come, knew what she had been asking him. She wanted him to say that he needed her to stay. And he hadn't said it. He had hurt Alice so much. Also he knew that without Alice around, Fiona would hurt too. And he was hurting himself—a detached part of his mind marvelled at how much he was hurting. What kind of fool would do something like this to himself?

It had been done delicately, but she had challenged him. *If you want me then you must ask me to stay. Otherwise I will go.* That was typical of her. He knew how tough-minded she could be, how determined to sort out a problem no matter what the cost might be.

He hadn't asked her to stay. Now he wondered if this had been cowardice on his part.

Had he made the right decision? Life with Alice could be so good, they could be a happy family of three—perhaps four or five in time. But then he remembered Melissa, his first marriage. No way was he going to risk a repetition of that. Better to be cautious. Be safe rather than risk being sorry.

But he was giving up so much.

Alice drove home somehow but had no recollection of the trip the next morning. She had a bath, a warm drink and then went straight to bed. She slept at once. It had always been this way in the past. If there was too much emotion, too much strain, after a while the body just cut off. She needed to sleep.

She slept well but woke quite early in the morning. This often happened, she loved the screaming of the gulls and the light through her curtains. Mysteriously, she felt quite calm. She thought about her visit to Ben the night before. Had she made a fool of herself? Perhaps yes, perhaps no. But whatever she had offered he had refused. He wouldn't ask her to stay. Well, he was entitled to make up his own mind.

Did she think he might change his mind? Was there still hope for her? Was that why he had asked her to wait for a fortnight before writing to the trust? She thought not. Ben had always been capable of making up his own mind. He didn't make important decisions lightly, but when he did he stuck by them. Alice remembered how she had felt about men when she'd come to Soalay, how she'd been so determined never to let a man into her life again. She should have been like Ben and stuck to her decision.

But now it was time to get up. She had a job to do.

CHAPTER TEN

HER day was quiet, which surprised her. She carried on with her ordinary work. It seemed odd that everything was so normal when her life had changed so radically the night before. And it had changed, she knew that. A set of half-realised hopes and dreams had been blown away, like the early morning mist on the mountaintops behind her. It would be a different life from now on. But that life had to go on.

At lunchtime there was something that she knew she had to do. She phoned Ben and asked if she could come over, there were a couple of things they had to consider. There was a child she wanted him to go out and visit and the suggestion of a talk to the pregnant mothers' group.

'Sure, come straight over,' Ben said. After a moment's hesitation he added, 'Have you time for a quick coffee?'

'I'd love one. But it'll really have to be quick. I've got a lot on this afternoon.' She didn't add that she didn't know just how long she could bear to be near him and pretend that nothing had happened.

But she knew that for a while she would have to

work with him, have to be near him. Better get the first meeting over quickly. So she went over and they discussed problems like the old friends and colleagues that they were. Nothing was said about the night before—though she could detect wariness in his eyes. Well, they could manage like this. They could talk to each other when it was necessary.

She didn't see him at all over the next two days. Sometimes it happened like this and they were never at the same place at the same time. And sometimes they never seemed to stop bumping into each other. But now…two days… Was he deliberately avoiding her? She didn't think so. Anyway, perhaps it was a good thing not to see too much of him, perhaps not necessary to see him. And the moment she thought this she knew what rubbish it was. If anything, she now missed him more than ever.

On the third day the weather matched her mood. Dark skies in the early morning, the first expected rattle of rain soon after that. And it went on and on. Just steady, unremitting rain. It wasn't a storm, there was no wind. But it seemed as if it would rain for ever. Well this was Soalay weather. It had happened before.

Alice had a clinic that afternoon but few people turned up. This was a day for staying at home and hoping that things would be better in the morning. Besides, the roads were impossible to walk down, the water overran the gutters, flooded across the pavements. Alice tidied her work room, caught up on her paperwork, stared dully out of the windows.

In the middle of the afternoon, a bit of excitement—

a message from Ben by way of his receptionist to hers. He would be out at the far, hilly side of the island for most of the rest of the day. He had been called to an accident. A car had skidded into a ravine and three people were badly injured. His surgery was cancelled. Alice shivered.

So, a dreary day with little to do. Perhaps tomorrow would be better, she'd have an early night and… She should have known better. Her phone rang.

A male voice, anxious, almost panicking. 'Midwife Muir? This is Malcolm Reay—you know, husband of Eleanor Reay over on Calvay Island? You've got to come, Eleanor has had a fall and she thinks the baby's coming. I can't bring her 'cos my car's at the garage and there's nobody here in the other cottages.'

'Malcolm! Calm down. First of all, how badly is Eleanor hurt?'

'She slipped on the front step in the rain. Her chest is bruised and she's cut her head. But she was shocked and that seems to have started things off early.'

'Why exactly does she think the baby's coming? Go and ask her.'

She heard muttering for a moment and then Malcolm returned and said, 'The waters have broken. And she's getting contractions.'

'Time them. How far apart are they?'

More mumbling, then, 'She says they're every ten minutes.'

'Right. Now, is she losing blood?'

'No. Well, just from her head. And she says that she

doesn't think she hurt the baby when she fell. It was just the shock of the fall that started it.'

'Right, that should give us some time. I'll set off now. Until then, keep her warm and comfortable. You know how to treat people for shock?'

'I know how to treat people for shock. I've been on a good first-aid course for men who work at sea. But it didn't cover delivering babies.'

'Just tell her you love her. That'll help no end. And I'm on my way.'

Alice stood a minute in thought. Eleanor Reay was now in week thirty-six—a four-week premature birth wasn't ideal but shouldn't present any real problems. And Eleanor had been a good mother-to-be, was strong, had shown no signs of any problems. It had only been a week since Alice had last visited her and had been enraptured by the new pictures Eleanor had drawn.

If there was time and she thought it possible, she would bring Eleanor back to the birthing unit. If it wasn't possible then Eleanor would have her home birth. Alice always had a full kit in her car, no problem there. All she needed to collect was her own wet-weather gear.

She phoned Ben's surgery number, left a message on his answering-machine, trying to keep her voice neutral. 'Hi, Ben, Alice here. It's half past six, I'm driving over to Calvay Island. Eleanor Reay has had a fall and gone into labour early. I might have to deliver at her home. I've got my mobile with me, if there are any problems I'll phone you. In fact, I'll report progress anyway. But don't worry, I don't expect any trouble. I'll probably be there overnight. Bye.' That should do, she thought.

Then she set off. They were the worst driving conditions she had ever been out in—worse even than when she and Ben had nearly fallen off the bridge into the stream. And then Ben had been driving. Now it was her turn. The one consolation was that there were few other vehicles on the roads. Everyone else had more sense.

Water was streaming across the road and her front wheels sent two great waves curving away on each side. She was glad of the height of her vehicle, glad of the four-wheel-drive. But she didn't feel safe and she didn't feel happy. She wished she hadn't had to come out.

As she got further into the countryside, the conditions got worse. Memories of her childhood crash came back to her, of being underwater. She sobbed quietly.

She didn't want to be out on her own, in weather like this. She wanted to be back in her own clinic. Perhaps Eleanor was really OK and she could come out in the morning. Stop thinking that way!

This could be much, much worse. Take things easy and all would be well. She pressed on.

And then she got to the causeway across to Calvay Island. And she realised what she had been doing. Somehow she had stopped herself thinking, had hidden the knowledge that this would be the worst, the most dangerous bit of the journey. But now she knew it. It was obvious.

She braked, stopped, looked through the greyness of the rain. It was high tide. And what made it worse was that the channel was narrow, and the rainwater and the streams feeding onto the channel had made the tide even higher. Waves were breaking right over the causeway.

And some of the causeway seemed to have crumbled and slipped in the sea! She couldn't cross this!

She'd have to wait. Perhaps go and find someone to take her across, someone with a better vehicle, who had more experience, who knew what they were doing. But as she looked she knew that was impossible. There was no one near. And Eleanor couldn't wait. And this was a first birth, it couldn't be handled by Malcolm. Eleanor needed a midwife, someone who knew what she was doing. Alice had to try to get across.

Sobbing, she let the car inch forward. Slowly, very slowly. It was hard because with the water washing across the narrow surface it was often almost impossible to see what was causeway and what was the sea. Once or twice she felt the wheels lose traction, felt the car slip to the side, but somehow she managed to correct it. She was getting there. She was progressing.

And eventually she was nearly there. She could see the road rising out of the water. Only a few more yards. Once there she'd be safe... Perhaps her concentration lapsed at the thought of safety. There was a thump as a wave hit the car. It seemed to shudder and she was skidding, slipping, sliding! The car was going to roll, it was turning on its side! Alice screamed with terror as her body was jerked painfully by her safety belt. For a moment she was a little girl of twelve again. She felt rather than heard the glass on her side window smash, and water poured into the car. She was cold, she was wet! She was going to drown, to die!

Vaguely she was aware of the car being pushed along on its side, she could hear or feel the grinding sound of it on the sea floor. Her head was nearly underwater and as she tried to scream again it splashed into her mouth so she coughed and was nearly sick. She was struggling but she couldn't move.

She had heard the old wives' tale that when you were about to die, your past life flashed through your mind. It didn't. But there was a vision that came back with astounding clarity. Perhaps the fear of impending death brought it on.

She had been working in an A and E department. She had attended a lecture given by a military doctor who had been on the front line of half a dozen of the nasty little wars that Britain somehow seemed to get involved in. For a moment, suspended in time, Alice could see and hear the man.

If you're in a bad situation and you panic, you triple the chances of dying. I once had to evacuate two dead soldiers who had been sheltering in an enemy house when it was hit by a shell and caught fire. Both ran to the nearest door, tried to open it. It was locked. They died desperately trying to kick the door down.

The doctor had paused, taken a drink of water. Then he'd gone on, *The door wasn't locked. They didn't realise it opened towards them. So—because they panicked—they died.*

Alice could remember the shock, the shiver of horror that had gone through the audience. So she wouldn't panic! Now, why was she drowning? Why was she not able to move? It was obvious! She reached down to her side and unfastened her safety belt. Then she pulled herself half-upright by clinging to the passenger seat.

She took a great breath, coughed and choked a moment, spat sea water out of her mouth. There was air here—and some light. She was not yet dead, there was hope.

Then she realised that the Land Rover had stopped grating along the seabed—and half of it wasn't under water. She wriggled a bit, managed to stand on what had been her door—and reached up to the passenger door. She unlocked it, threw it back. Then she hoisted herself upwards—and the top half of her body was out in the rain.

The car was now still. It had beached in a little cove, some distance from the causeway. Water was rushing past it but she thought if she got out she could scramble ashore. She started to climb out, ignoring the scratches, the bruises. She was going to survive!

Then she thought. She was here to do a job. She muttered a quick prayer. Slid back into the half-water-filled car. She somehow negotiated her way to the back, grabbed the three bags she knew that she was most likely to need. It was agonising—wriggling, bending, pulling—but she managed to coax them out. And all the time there was the fear that the water might suddenly get stronger, drag the Land Rover into the current and drown her.

But it didn't. She leaned out of the opened door and threw the bags one by one onto the little beach. Then she slid down the side of the vehicle and was up to her waist in water. The passing water plucked at her but she managed to wade ashore.

She was wet through, chilled to the bone, bruised, cut and battered. She calculated that she was a mile from her patient and no one knew where she was. Well, she'd have to do what she could. She felt in her pocket for her mobile. It might be wet but it could work. Not a chance—it must have been smashed when the car had rolled over.

Three bags on shore. She stuffed two under a rock and picked up the most important one. Then she set off to walk to Eleanor's cottage. She had a baby to deliver.

'Look at the state of you! Are you all right? Have you had an accident?' Malcolm was at the cottage door, mouth and eyes wide open.

'Yes, I've had an accident.' Alice walked past him, talking as she moved. 'I want a quick five minutes with Eleanor and then I'll need to borrow some clothes from her. And if I could have a bath, I think that would be a good idea. Oh, and, Malcolm. A hot drink would be welcome.' Nothing like getting your priorities right, she thought.

She knew where to go and went straight to the ground-floor bedroom where Eleanor was to give birth. She was aware that a dripping-wet midwife wasn't exactly ideal but she wanted a swift preliminary look before taking time to look after herself. However, the first glance told her that Eleanor was not yet in any desperate state. 'How are you, Eleanor?'

'I seem to be better than you,' Eleanor said. 'At the moment I'm uncomfortable but not in any great pain. The contractions are getting closer together. But I can wait till you're in a fit state to be a proper midwife. And then you can tell me what happened.'

She pointed across the bedroom. 'Underwear in the top drawer. In that wardrobe you'll find a top and a pair of slacks that should just fit. And there's some slippers there, too. Malcolm!' she shouted.

Malcolm appeared at the door. 'Run the bath, find a couple of towels. Make the midwife a mug of tea and a sandwich. Oh, and get her a dram—just a wee one.'

'Right,' said Malcolm. He had recognised that whoever was in charge here, it wasn't him.

Alice hesitated. She didn't like leaving her patient but she knew she'd do a better job when she was clean and warm and dry. No way did she want to examine someone when she was wet through and coated with sand. So she said, 'Scream if you need me. I'll be as quick as I can.' She seized clothes from where she had been directed, headed towards the sound of running water.

She undressed in the bathroom, threw her sodden clothes into a basket. She scanned her naked body. She hadn't realised just how badly bruised and scratched she was. Still, it may be painful but it was only minor stuff. Adrenaline still coursed through her body so she could cope. Later, she knew, it would all hurt more and she would feel desperately tired. But now she had a job to do.

Her bath was quickly over—though she would have loved to lie there, luxuriating.

She pulled on Eleanor's clothes, walked into the bedroom to find tea and a giant pile of sandwiches waiting for her. Malcolm obviously thought that it wasn't possible to over-cater. There was also a bottle of malt whisky and a glass. Alice looked at them and sighed. 'We'll both have a drop of that when you're a father,' she told Malcolm. 'But I'll not touch it until then.' She told him where her other two medical bags were hidden, asked him to fetch them. He set off at once. Then Alice turned to Eleanor. 'Now, for the business of the evening,' she said. 'Let's have a look at how baby is coming along.'

At first it was a straightforward labour. Eleanor had been a perfect patient, she had done everything asked of her—correct diet, exercise, relaxation practice. There should be no trouble. Alice completed the usual initial tests—listened to the foetal heartbeat, took the blood pressure, pulse and temperature. All carefully entered in the notes. Then there was an internal examination. 'Well-dilated cervix,' Alice told Eleanor. 'Everything going fine so far.' Eleanor smiled.

Malcolm returned, carrying the two extra bags. Then he needed to wash and change and after that came in to hold Eleanor's hand. Eleanor carried on with the breathing and relaxation exercises she had practised so often before.

Alice was happy with Eleanor's progress. She knew that she was not fully fit and inside her there was vast fatigue. It would be good to get to bed herself—but until the baby was safely born, she could cope.

The baby's head crowned. Alice put her hand on the head, then motioned for Malcolm to come round for the first glimpse of his child. He peered at the tiny rounded skull, the few strands of damp hair, and Alice thought she saw tears in his eyes.

'I want to feel,' said Eleanor, and reached down to touch. 'That's my baby,' she said, and Alice thought she had never seen such a smile on a mother's face.

As the baby's head was visible on the perineum, the

rest of the body should continue its descent. Alice looked down then she frowned. At the next contraction the head appeared to retract instead of coming out a little further. She said nothing, but uneasily waited for a further contraction. The same thing happened. It was called the turtle sign.

She fought to keep calm, the last thing she needed was to alarm Eleanor. But something in her attitude must have disturbed the mother. 'Is everything all right?' Eleanor called. There was tension in her voice.

'Baby's too happy where it is. Doesn't want to come out into the cold wicked world. No need to worry,' Alice reassured her, and waited for the next contraction. If she had been in a hospital this was when she would have called for the obstetric registrar and a paediatrician. But she was on her own. She could cope, she had to.

No doubt about it. The baby was making no progress. Shoulder dystocia, Alice guessed. After the head appeared, all babies had to rotate as they were being born. One shoulder at a time appeared. Sometimes, perhaps if it was a very large baby, a shoulder became trapped.

'I want you further down the bed,' Alice told Eleanor. And I want you in the lithotomy position. That means you pull your knees up to your chest and then spread them as wide as you can. Then I'm going to give you a quick injection and an episiotomy. We'll just give baby a bit more space.'

'It's shoulder dystocia, isn't it?' Eleanor panted. 'But you can deal with it, can't you?'

For a moment Alice wondered if it was such a good

idea to prepare mothers-to-be by making them read about all that just could happen, as well as all that would happen.

'It could be dystocia,' she said, making her voice sound cheerful. 'No need to worry. I've dealt with plenty of them before.' She ignored the little voice that told her that in the past she had always had help.

First, she performed the episiotomy. 'Malcolm, come down here. Put your hand there.' Looking worried, Malcolm did as he was told. Alice positioned his hand on Eleanor's abdomen. Then she placed her hand on top of it, pressed downwards. 'Hold your hand there with just that pressure. Don't move it till I tell you.'

Malcolm said nothing but did as he was told. He didn't look at what Alice was doing, but turned his head and smiled—somehow—at his wife. Alice knew she was lucky. Many fathers would have panicked at this stage.

Carefully, she drew the baby's head upwards, then with the other hand reached in and slid four fingers behind the posterior shoulder. Ease the shoulder round! At first she thought it wouldn't happen but then it slipped into the hollow of the sacrum. Then the shoulder was delivered. 'Right,' said Alice. 'Small emergency over. Now everything will go according to plan.'

And it did.

The baby girl was born at one in the morning. A fine, healthy, large girl. There was the Apgar test to perform, the usual post-birth tasks and the notes to write up, but now Alice knew that the job was largely done.

The baby was to be called Joanna. Alice learned that Eleanor and Malcolm had debated names for hours.

Alice remembered that she had just started to think about names for the child that she had never had. She had rather fancied Kate. Now she had her private moment of sadness for her own miscarried child. This always happened but it soon passed. This was a happy time.

She was kissed by Malcolm, agreed at last to share a dram with him. Then there was the usual settling-down process for Eleanor and soon she and her baby in the cot by her side were asleep. Malcolm was to sleep in the armchair drawn up at his wife's bedside. Alice knew that he wouldn't sleep much. He could hardly take his eyes off his new child.

In her turn Alice knew what she herself had to do then. Lie down before she collapsed. She rejected a bed in the upstairs bedroom, said she would sleep on the couch in the living room, that Malcolm was to call her if there was any problem at all. And she only intended to doze for a couple of hours.

She didn't bother getting undressed. She would just sleep for a while. In the past she'd stayed awake for much longer than this. But the moment she shut her eyes she was conscious of a vast fatigue. She slept at once.

What was the noise? It was ridiculous, it would wake up the baby! A hammering, rattling, banging kind of noise—some kind of machinery? What was it? After a moment it died away but she could still hear it in the distance.

She was still on the couch in the living room but mysteriously it had become light. A typical change in the island weather—she could see the sun shining. She looked at her watch and blinked. Two hours' sleep? It was six o'clock, she had slept for five hours. Well, better get up and look at her new baby and her mother… And another noise! Someone was hammering at the front door, a frantic knocking. Didn't they know that people needed to sleep?

Alice stumbled to open the door, her bare feet chilled on the stone floor. And there was Ben.

Ben? What was he doing here at this hour of the morning? And why was he looking so wild-eyed? And why was he wearing some kind of an all-in-one suit and a helmet?

He looked at her disbelievingly. Then he grabbed her, pulled her to him, pressed kisses all over her face. His voice was desperate. 'Alice! You're alive!'

'Well, yes,' she said.

Malcolm came to the door to join them. 'I heard the helicopter,' he said. 'Shall I put the kettle on?'

CHAPTER ELEVEN

MALCOLM took silence to mean assent, so he went to put
on the kettle. And Alice could have stayed there for
ever, being kissed by Ben. She felt at home, comfortable, as if she was in the place where it was obvious she
ought to be. And she doubted if Ben would ever let her
go. Certainly, he showed no signs of it. But slowly she
became aware of how cold her feet were, of the cuts and
bruises on her body, of the immense fatigue she still felt.
But she didn't care. She was being kissed by Ben and
it was marvellous.

He was looking at her with an expression she had
never seen before—a mixture of wonderment and joy.
'You seem happy,' she said.

There was an infinity of desolation in his voice. 'I
thought you were dead,' he said. 'I knocked on this door
to ask for help in looking for your body and you
answered. Alice, I still can't believe it.'

'Well, I'm not dead. Though I have felt better in my
time.'

And then somehow the doctor in him took over. 'You
don't look good,' he said. 'But since you're standing and

talking, I presume you're all right for the moment. Now, what's this about a baby?'

'She's asleep,' Malcolm said, beaming as he reappeared. 'But come and look if you like.'

'I would like. And, Alice, you go straight back to bed.'

'But I'm the midwife here. It's my birth.'

'No. For the moment I'm the doctor and you're my patient so I'm in charge.'

'Well, you're not to make any decisions about Joanna unless I agree.' Alice felt sulky. Her authority was being taken from her and she didn't like it.

'You'll be part of any decision-making.'

'Good. So long as that's understood.' Then she found that she was swaying and she needed Ben's strong arm round her to ease her back to her bed on the couch.

Things did slip just a little out of her control then. She watched, half-bemused as, after examining Eleanor and Joanna, Ben arranged for Eleanor, Malcolm and baby Joanna to be airlifted to the mainland hospital so Joanna and her mother could be checked properly.

That decision having been taken, he came to Alice and said, 'Your turn now. You can tell me later exactly what happened, I just want to see how you are.'

'Right, Doctor.'

It was just a quick examination but he told her that he needed to look at all her cuts and bruises. This involved his looking at her naked body. With a half-suppressed giggle she saw that he was being as distant, as doctorly as possible. Nothing he said or did indicated that he was aware that she was an attractive young woman, In fact, one that he had… Well, perhaps that was how it should be, but still… 'Thank you, Doctor,' she said sweetly when he had finished, and pulled the blanket up round her. 'That was just like being examined by a machine.'

'Don't you dare push it,' he growled, and for a moment he was the old Ben again. 'You're a bit battered but as far as I can see there's nothing seriously wrong with you that a lot of sleep won't cure. I don't think there's any need for you to go to the mainland hospital, though perhaps…'

'I'm not going. I've got work to do.' Then she wondered how she was going to get back. 'Anyway, what are you going to do? Going to the mainland as well?'

'No. There's a council team that will have to come out and look at the causeway, and the police will be here too. If Eleanor and Malcolm don't mind, you and I can wait here till help comes.'

'I don't think they'll mind,' Alice said with a grin. She guessed that, like many islanders, the couple wouldn't even lock their door when they left.

She still needed Ben's arm to steady her as she went to say goodbye to Eleanor and the baby. Eleanor said she would have been just as happy to stay and be looked after by Alice. Then the Medivac team brought in stretchers, Ben went out to supervise and shortly afterwards there was the roar and clatter of engines and the helicopter was on its way.

Ben came back into the living room and she wondered, what next? They were alone together, would be alone for some hours. Why was Ben looking at her in that way, as if there was something that he couldn't quite believe?

'You're still exhausted,' he said to her. 'Stay there and rest and I'll make you some breakfast. Eleanor was most insistent on that. But now lie back on the couch and try to sleep.'

'I'm all right now.'

'Lie down and rest! Doctor's orders.'

So she did as he'd commanded. Then he came to her, leaned over her. Tenderly, he took her head in his two hands, stared down at her. 'You are beautiful.' he said, 'but more than that, you are you. Living, breathing, sweet Alice Muir. Not two hours ago I thought that you were dead and my life seemed to fall apart.'

She looked up at him and saw something she had never expected to see. Tears? Ben crying for her?

He kissed her gently, then sat on the floor beside her couch and took hold of her hand. He held it inside his shirt so she could feel the uneven beat of his heart. 'First thing, tell me what happened. I need to know, to make sense of things.'

'Why did you think I was dead?' She was curious.

'Well, I first got your phone message very early this morning. Didn't get back from the accident till then. And I was worried. It was evil weather, a bad journey and possibly a difficult birth when you arrived. Then I couldn't raise you on your mobile and the storm had apparently brought down the landline here. So you were marooned. I didn't know what help you might need. That's when I decided to order out the helicopter. But when I flew here, I saw the damage to the causeway. Then I saw your car, on its side, in the water. There was no sign of you. The pilot flew up and down a while…'

His voice faltered. 'Looking for a body. But we gave up hope. Then he flew here. And the best thing that has ever happened to me happened then. I thought you were dead and there you were—alive.'

Yes, she thought. Those were definitely tears.

He was silent a while and then said, 'So tell me what happened to you.'

So she told him. The callout from Malcolm, the causeway being flooded. The Land Rover sliding off the edge of the causeway and being carried along until it beached and her feverish attempts to escape.

'I thought I was going to die,' she told him. 'I panicked. But somehow I got a grip on myself and after that…' she shrugged '…well, it wasn't too hard.'

She saw him wince as she told her story. 'If I'd known,' he muttered. 'If only I'd known.'

She smiled up at him. 'Don't worry. Ultimately we got a happy ending. The birth was a bit of trouble—shoulder dystocia—but now mother and child are fine and I'll soon get over a few scratches and bruises.' Then she thought of something, a new worry. 'Ben, what about my Land Rover?'

Ben obviously couldn't have cared less about it. He shrugged. 'Who cares? I'll phone the garage, get it pulled out, they'll order you another one. The important thing is that you are all right. We'll let the trust sort out what needs—'

Suddenly, he sounded alarmed, his body tensed. 'The trust! Alice, have you written to them saying that you'd take the job they offered you on the mainland?'

She hesitated. Did she want him to know? 'No,' she

said. 'I thought I might think...think if there might still be something for me here.'

She saw him relax and he leaned forward and kissed her again. 'I hope there is,' he said. 'Alice, when I saw your Land Rover in the water, when I thought that you might be dead...'

She watched as he shook his head disbelievingly. He went on, 'All the time you've been back on Soalay memories have been coming back. Of what we did and what we meant to each other fifteen years ago. But then they became more than memories! We were living in the present, we were different people, and what I started to feel for you was far greater than any schoolboy crush! And then I remembered that just a few days ago I had told you to leave, that we had no future. Alice, I just didn't know what I was giving up! A future without you? And then I thought what a coward I had been. I was just too scared to take a risk. But you had risked your life...probably lost your life doing something to help someone.'

'Ben! It doesn't matter. Don't get upset. We all make decisions that are sometimes wrong!'

'Sometimes really big mistakes.' He looked at her as-sessingly, and then smiled. 'How do you feel now?'

How did she feel? Well, happy. Happier than she'd thought she could ever be. But there was something else. 'You're not going to believe this,' she said. 'That was a lovely, lovely thing that you just said to me. But how do I feel now? Well, when he first saw you Malcolm said he was going to put the kettle on, but nothing much happened after that. Ben, right now what I need most is a mug of tea.'

'And I call myself a doctor,' he muttered. 'I should have known.'

Malcolm had left all that was necessary for breakfast out on the kitchen table. Ben put most of it away. He decided that the traditional full English breakfast was not quite what Alice needed. But he'd make her some toast and the requested mug of tea. In fact, he rather fancied a mug of tea himself.

As he was alone for a minute, it was a chance for him to take stock, to think what had happened to him over the past couple of hours. In that short time he had felt the depths of despair and then ecstasy. When he had seen the empty vehicle, half-full of water, he had been certain that Alice was dead. He could still remember the bleakness of his imagined future. What would life be like without her? And then he had discovered that she was alive! How many men got a second chance at happiness? Well, he knew what he had to do now.

Putting tea and toast onto a tray, he walked back into the living room, sat again on the floor by the couch. He took her hand again, kissed it. 'Alice, there's something I want to say to you,' he said.

Alice didn't reply.

Ben frowned, looked at her. There was a tiny smile on her face but her breathing was heavy and her chest was rising and falling in an unmistakable rhythm. Ben sighed. No time for passionate declarations now. Alice was firmly, soundly, definitely asleep.

Ben walked outside, took out his mobile. 'Sergeant Cullen? Dr Cavendish here. There's some organising I'd like you to do…'

Alice decided that it was nice not to have to do anything, not to have to make any decisions, just to lie there, sleep when she wanted, and let other people do everything necessary. And there did seem to be a lot of people around, supervised by Sergeant Cullen. Even a tow truck to pull her Land Rover out of the sea.

Somehow, Ben's vehicle had arrived outside the cottage. She was bundled into it, the seat reclined, a blanket wrapped round her. Well, she'd sleep some more.

She was taken to Taighean dhe Gaoithe. She tried to suggest that she ought to go to her own flat, that she had work to do. 'Morag will deal with all your appointments for the next couple of days,' Ben told her. 'You're in no fit state to work. And you need looking after.'

Alice didn't feel like arguing. She had a bath, breakfast provided by a horrified Mrs McCann and then, of all places, was ushered into Ben's bedroom and Ben's double bed. 'I haven't made up your old bed,' Mrs McCann told her. 'And the doctor told me that you were to sleep here. He said to tell you that he has to go into town, there's a lot of things to organize, but that he'll be back as soon as possible.'

'Right,' said Alice. Let other people make the decisions. She would sleep.

* * *

'What are you doing in my daddy's bed?'

When she woke up Alice felt so much better. Her body ached from the assorted scratches and bruises but her mind was wonderfully clear. She peered at Fiona, who was looking at her curiously from the side of the bed. 'I had…an accident,' she said, 'but I'm all right now. Your daddy said I could stay here for a while.'

'I like it when you stay. Can I get into bed with you? Sometimes my daddy lets me get into bed with him.'

'I'd love you to get into bed with me.'

Fiona climbed in. 'I've brought a book,' she explained, 'just in case it's necessary.'

'Then we'd better read it together,' Alice said.

It was very pleasant, sitting in bed, reading to Fiona. Alice was almost sorry when the door opened and Ben came in. Almost sorry. 'And what's happening here?' Ben asked.

'We're sitting in bed, reading,' Fiona explained. She wriggled sideways. 'There's room for you if you want to get in. Then we can all read.'

'It's an attractive offer but I don't think I will just now. In fact, Mrs McCann has got your tea ready. I think you ought to go down to the kitchen.'

'All right. Is Auntie Alice staying the night?'

'I hope so. If she wants to.'

'I'd like to stay,' said Alice. 'Fiona, I'll see you later.'

Fiona scampered along the corridor. Ben closed the door after her, then came to the bedside, took Alice's head in his hands and kissed her. 'I'll be a doctor first and then a lover,' he said. 'How do you feel?'

'I feel good. All I needed was a sleep. Ben, there's a lot of things I need to—'

'Tomorrow. Everything is fine, nothing needs doing before tomorrow. Incidentally, I heard from the mainland hospital. Young Joanna Reay is doing fine, Eleanor too.'

'That's good. Ben, what am I doing here? I could have gone to my own flat.'

He kissed her again, then kicked off his shoes and stretched out on the bed by her side. He took her hand. 'You know, for two apparently intelligent people we haven't been very bright, have we?'

'How haven't we been very bright?'

'We nearly parted. Again. After fifteen years we had a second chance and we nearly missed it. I suppose it was my fault. I just didn't have the sense to realise that having made one mistake didn't mean that I would make another. No way could you be another Melissa.'

'I hope not. And no way could you be another Sean. That was so obvious!'

He stretched his arm round her, pulled her closer to him. 'So we both made mistakes. And now they're behind us. Good.'

He kissed her yet again. 'Next problem. What about your high-flying career in London? What about the vast salary you might earn?'

'Ben! The last thing I want to be is a high-flyer! I don't want to spend all my life behind a desk, telling other people what to do. I'm a midwife, I like delivering babies. I like talking to mums-to-be. And as for living in

London… Well, I'm afraid I've gone off the idea. After this time in Soalay, I know I never want to leave.'

'We first met here,' he said. 'We first fell in love here—and it was love.'

'It was indeed. But…now it's different. What I feel for you is somehow deeper. There's more to me now than there was when I was eighteen. And there's more to you too.'

This time a much, much longer kiss.

'Oh, Ben that's so wonderful!' she gasped.

'When we are married we can do it every night and every morning,' he whispered.

'When we are married! Ben, you've forgotten something. A lady needs to be asked.'

'Of course.' His face was so close to hers now and she could see that he was not joking. 'Alice, I realised that life without you would be nothing. I need you and I want you and I love you. Oh, and I come as a package. Take me and you take Fiona. And she loves you too. So will you marry me?'

'Of course I will! I've wanted to marry you for over fifteen years now. Now, can you carry on with what you were doing for a while…?'

MILLS & BOON

MEDICAL™
On sale 1st May 2009

THE SURGEON SHE'S BEEN WAITING FOR
by Joanna Neil

Attraction sparkles between career-focused A&E doctor Megan
and gorgeous surgeon Theo. Theo, however, is facing his
greatest challenge yet – looking after his five-year-old nephew.
Megan doesn't believe in happy ever after, but Theo and little
Harry steal her heart…for the first time she finds
herself imagining a future – and a family!

THE BABY DOCTOR'S BRIDE
by Jessica Matthews

Children's doctor Ivy Harris seeks urgent help from
ex-paediatrician Ethan Locke. Brooding Ethan's given up on
children and women, yet Ivy is irresistible! Before he'll feel
whole again there's something he must do. Ivy can only
pray that he'll come back to make her his bride…

THE MIDWIFE'S NEW-FOUND FAMILY
by Fiona McArthur

Attempting to bury the memory of single father
Dr Ben Moore, midwife Misty sets off for a new life in
Lyrebird Lake – only to discover the new locum has familiar
blue eyes! Will the magical setting rekindle that magical
moment between Misty and Ben?

THE ROYAL HOUSE OF KAREDES

Two crowns, two islands, one legacy

Volume One
BILLIONAIRE PRINCE,
PREGNANT MISTRESS
by Sandra Marton

Wanted for her body – and her baby!

Aspiring New York jewellery designer Maria Santo has come to Aristo to win a royal commission.

Cold, calculating and ruthless, Prince Xander Karedes beds Maria, thinking she's only sleeping with him to save her business.

So when Xander discovers Maria's pregnant, he assumes it's on purpose. What will it take for this billionaire prince to realise he's falling in love with his pregnant mistress…?

Available 17th April 2009

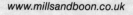

2 FREE

BOOKS AND A SURPRISE GIFT!

We would like to take this opportunity to thank you for reading this Mills & Boon® book by offering you the chance to take TWO more specially selected titles from the Medical™ series absolutely FREE! We're also making this offer to introduce you to the benefits of the Mills & Boon® Book Club™—

- ★ **FREE home delivery**
- ★ **FREE gifts and competitions**
- ★ **FREE monthly Newsletter**
- ★ **Exclusive Mills & Boon Book Club offers**
- ★ **Books available before they're in the shops**

Accepting these FREE books and gift places you under no obligation to buy, you may cancel at any time, even after receiving your free shipment. Simply complete your details below and return the entire page to the address below. You don't even need a stamp!

YES! Please send me 2 free Medical books and a surprise gift. I understand that unless you hear from me, I will receive 4 superb new titles every month for just £2.99 each, postage and packing free. I am under no obligation to purchase any books and may cancel my subscription at any time. The free books and gift will be mine to keep in any case.

M9ZED

Ms/Mrs/Miss/Mr ....Initials ....

BLOCK CAPITALS PLEASE

Surname ....

Address ....

....

....Postcode..............................

Send this whole page to:
UK: FREEPOST CN81, Croydon, CR9 3WZ